UPGRADED BY THE TRILLEST THUG

YONA

Cole Hart
SIGNATURE NOVELS

Upgraded By The Trillest Thug

Copyright © 2021 by Yona

Mailing List

To stay up to date on new releases, plus get information on contests, sneak peeks, and more,

Go To The Website Below...

www.colehartsignature.com

1.3.17 --- 1.15.17
Brooklyn Faith Ellison, I miss you more than words can explain, and I honestly thought about you a whole lot writing this book. I wish that sickness didn't hit you, but it did. With time the pain is easier to deal with, but the crazy ache of needing you with me is still there. I love you, Brookie...

8.2.95 ---- 10.7.20

Darrell, bro, this one still hurts; it's still fresh. To see you how I last saw you was never the plan. We were supposed to get rich and pop bottles together; just know the plan is to still make it, you just not here with me anymore. You will always be my favorite little cousin, though you forever were my baby brother!

To my readers, thank you for sticking by me no matter what. The support doesn't go unnoticed.

❧ 1 ❧

DENVER

Feeling the small slaps on my face, I opened my eyes and looked at my baby girl, Dakota. Drool was falling from her mouth onto my face as she kissed me. I frowned a little because I had finally been able to fall asleep, and now, she was back up. My baby wasn't the one who slept all night, being as though I let her sleep when she wanted and wasn't sure how to put her on a schedule. Sitting up, I lifted her up and tossed her in the air, causing her to laugh and myself to smile. Dakota's dad was someone I didn't care to speak on. He was killed a few weeks after I gave birth to her, and I was fine with that. Not that I wished death on anybody, but he was the type of person that had it coming to him. Honest to God, I was happy it was him and not me. Though we were only fifteen at the time my baby girl came into this world, that boy had developed a serious hand problem. What always got me was he was quick to put his hands on his handicapped mom and me, but not his abusive ass daddy. At first, I wanted a boy; however, when they told me Dakota was a girl, my heart smiled. Seeing how they passed down the trait of being women beaters, I didn't want a son who would develop that habit.

Life was hard for me, and it wasn't just because I had a baby early on and had to take care of her myself. My mother, Treasure Martin, was serious when she told me, "You better take that baby to school with you. I'm not raising nobody else baby when I don't want to raise my own." She stood by that shit every day. The only help I did have was the welfare office and selling some of my WIC checks. Treasure gave me enough to get my baby some milk, clothes, and get her to doctor's appointments. Other than that, I barely saw her ass. Daycare wasn't an option because Treasure didn't have time to take me to do the necessary paper-work, so dropping out of school to watch my baby was the best thing. Of course, her other grandmother wanted to be there, but her interactions with her were limited. For one, she was still with her no-good, abusive ass husband, and her movements were limited due to the wheelchair he had put her in. So, every other week I would take Dakota over to visit while her grandpop was out playing card games and drinking with his friends.

Hard knocks on the door caused me to jump, startling me. The way the knocks were, it sounded like the police were about to come storming through at any moment. Instead of going to see who it was, I closed my door and locked it. Treasure ain't play that coming over without calling shit, and by the knocks, I was sure whoever it was didn't call, or she would have already had the door unlocked for them.

"Who the fuck is it, and why the fuck are you banging on my god damn door? It's five in the damn morning, you had to have lost your rabbit ass mind," I heard my mom screaming while the locks where being undone.

It was quiet for a while, so I went back to playing with my daughter. Blowing on her stomach, we both giggled. Dakota looked just like me, light-skin, gray eyes, sandy-brown, curly hair, and chunky cheeks with the matching dimple in our left cheek.

"Oouuu, mama's baby needs her butt changed." I tickled her while grabbing a pamper and the wipes. After changing her, I scooped her up to go throw away the pamper and make her another bottle.

Opening my room door, I came face to face with a lady and a few cops behind her standing at the front door. She looked at me with a small smile, and something told me the bitch wasn't here for a friendly meeting.

"Hi, I'm Hannah, I work for DHS. We got an anonymous call about you and the baby's living condition. I'm sure you know this place isn't in a great condition to have you and the child in," she said as she looked around.

I looked around with her like it was my first time seeing things as well. My eyes traveled to the trash bag that was taped to the window, thanks to Treasure messing with somebody's man and the lady came and said, "Now you got a permanent air conditioner for that nasty ass house. Bitch need to let some fresh air up in that hot muthafucka." I knew it was that lady who called, because she always threw threats about calling.

The counters were covered with empty beer cans, E&J apple bottles, cigarettes, and chocolate Dutch guts. Along with dirty dishes, roaches, and whatever else crawled in here. The couches were sinking in and covered with a trash bag because the bed bugs were bad, they were eating us alive. I was kind of glad we were getting out of here.

"We are going to take you both down to the children's hospital to get checked out, and from there we will contact the biological father, and since your mom can't get the baby, we will go for his mother if we can't get in contact with him. Do you have information for them?" she asked me.

"Her dad passed away a few months back, and his mother is wheelchair bound. We can't stay together? You have not said anything about where I would be placed. Wherever I go, my baby can't go?" I questioned.

The happy feeling I just felt about finally getting out of here moments ago was gone. My stomach began to hurt, and I was fighting back tears. There was no way my baby could be separated from me. None of this was my fault and should not affect me. Holding my baby tight to me, I pleaded with her for my baby to stay with me.

"Baby, this isn't how it works. I wish there was something I could do, but that would only be if your father or his family takes you both. Now, please get you both some things. And let us go," she said sternly.

My first mind was to knock her ass out and make a run for it. Unlike my mother, I wasn't a fighter though, so the thought quickly left as fast as it came. I wasn't a punk either, so if you hit me then we could get it going, but if not, my ass would walk away. A lot of people took advantage of the fact that I would sit there and allow a person to curse me out, call me names, and everything else and wouldn't blink. That was because it wasn't shit a person could say about me that I didn't already know. I was always all kinds of hoes because Herron made everybody in the hood he was fucking before he died believe that I was sleeping with the entire neighborhood when I slept with him and only him, and not because I wanted to. If I didn't, he would beat my ass until I did. He ain't tell that part though.

Dragging my feet, I held on to my baby with one hand and used my other to go get her bins. She had one where I stored her milk, baby food, and bottles. The other was her clothes. Once I pulled it into the living room. One of the cops came and carried it outside. I then went back and got my small bin. The moment I stepped back into the living room, I locked eyes with Treasure, who looked like she didn't have a care in the world. She was leaned against the wall, smoking her cigarette like they were there for a friendly visit. After they made sure we had our stuff, they walked me outside.

"Don't be no weak bitch, we don't do that crying shit," my mom said as I made my way out of the door.

In front of her, I held my tears in, but once we got into that car, I broke down. My baby was going to be taken away from me, and it wasn't shit I could do. I imagined us getting up out that house one day, but not us being separated. Dakota must have felt my sadness, because she started to cry. I rocked her and shushed her until she calmed down. We made it to the hospital, and I was dreading walking inside with these people. Once we were in the room, they made phone calls and whatever else they had to do. While Dakota slept in my arms, they kept coming to ask was I hungry or did I need anything. My answer was the same each time, no. The only help I needed was for them to find someone to keep me and my baby together.

"We found a family member on the dad's side who is willing to take in the baby only. It is in our best interest to keep the child in the family. You, on the other hand, we couldn't get into contact with anyone, and your mom refused to give us any information on your father. Do you have any on him? He and his family are our last resort before the baby is taken to the home of the great aunt, and you will be going to one of our group homes," the same lady who came and ruined my life said.

I shook my head no, and she gave me a sad look. I knew what was coming, but I wasn't prepared for it. She reached her hands out for my baby, and I lost it.

"No, no, please. Don't take her from me. She's all I have, please, I'll do anything." I held on to Dakota as tight as I possibly could without hurting her.

I could taste my tears mixed with snot as I screamed and begged for them to not take her. My cries woke Dakota up, and she began to cry too. A few other people came in and asked me to calm down as they all but pried my baby out of my hands, making me cry harder. I tried to run out of the room behind them, but someone held me.

"If you don't calm down, we will have to sedate you," the nurse said, but I didn't care. My entire world was being snatched away from me. Sliding down the wall, I held onto my knees and let out gut-wrenching screams.

"This isn't fair, I took care of her. I loved her the best that I could. All I wanted was to be the mom to her that I never had, and y'all taking it away from me and telling me to calm down. How? How can I calm down?" I sobbed.

My sobbing quickly turned into me trying to catch my breath. The nurse sat next to me and rubbed my back, telling me to breathe and to relax, as if she could understand my pain. The nurse lifted my head and pulled out a mirror, forcing me to look at myself. Tears were streaming down my face, my eyes were puffy, and snot was covering my lips and all over my face.

"Remember the look on your face and tell yourself you will not be this person. You are better than this person. I know the circumstances are messed up, baby girl, but you must fight, and fight until you can't no more. Don't drop your head, do what you must do to get that little beautiful baby back. You still have a chance. They see you in here acting crazy, baby, that'll only cause more harm than good," she said before pulling me into a hug.

Her words hit my heart and had me feeling a tiny bit better. Yet nothing could lift my spirits in this moment. Since the day my child was born, we hadn't spent this much time apart, and I didn't know what to do now that we were. I felt a lot of things in my life that were not good; however, this was the first time I felt defeated, and I wasn't sure if I could come back from this, though I would try my hardest to. My life had taken a turn for the worst, and it didn't look like brighter days were going to come.

❧ 2 ❧

ZAMIR

Watching my aunt take her last breath should have been a weak moment for me; instead, it wasn't. I had been preparing myself for this moment for years. She had lung cancer, and watching her battle for as long as she did made me see life in a different way than most eighteen-year-olds. Monica had prepared me on what to do after this moment. Auntie ain't have no life insurance and the only thing she owned was her house. My cousin, Mikey, her son, would get her house, but I was to stay in it until I didn't want to anymore. She looked out for me because both my mom and dad were somewhere with AIDS, strung out on whatever drug they decided to do. I never got the chance to meet them. I often used to ask about them, and Aunt Monica told me as much as she could, and even though she held no punches, she kept in mind to remind me that parents fuck up, yet that doesn't mean they don't love you. For the most part, I knew nothing about them besides what they used to do before the drugs, and I was okay with it. I was glad my aunt raised me, because I didn't want anything to do with them just like they didn't want anything to do with me. It was by the grace of God they got that shit after they had me and I was living with my aunt. Had I been exposed to something so life threatening, I probably would have killed them and myself the moment I was old enough to grab a gun.

I held on to my aunt's hand until it was no longer warm. My big cousin had long ago stormed out of the room. He couldn't take seeing his mother take her last breath, and he damn sure didn't want to see her lifeless. I was the complete opposite. I wanted to be there for every moment, just like she had always been there for me. So, I sat there with a solemn expression when they pulled the plug. It took about three minutes for her to take her last breath. That was about forty minutes ago. The fucked-up thing was, we had no way to bury her. My auntie struggled taking care of us when we were kids. She worked two jobs just to make ends meet. When cancer hit her, it hit hard, and the only check that was being brought into the house was a disability check. Which was why I having no problem hitting the streets and trying to get the money as fast as I could, to help her anyway.

I thought about calling my brother, Manny. We were not blood, but you couldn't tell us that shit. I knew his parents could help us out and would do so without blinking an eye. Just like my aunt, they played a big role in my life. My big cousin's pride was too big, and he would flip if he knew I had gone to them for money.

Seeing my aunt laid there with no signs of life and a possible chance that the state would have to bury her hurt me to the core. I honestly thought I was numb to pain; however, this tugged at my heart. I would switch places with her, with no second thoughts. I was worthless to this world while she meant everything. My eyes burned and I chewed on my lip. I could feel myself about to break down. Standing up, I kissed my aunt's cold forehead, and using a tissue, I wiped what looked like blood mixed with water from her nose, then tossed it in the trash. Walking back over to her, I took a deep breath and let it out. There was no way I was leaving without saying goodbye.

"I love you, baby girl. I will see you one day, hopefully soon.

Watch over me, because I'm gone need you now more than ever. You know your boy about to hit these streets and hit them hard. I ain't got shit and I ain't about to be out here like that. Thank you for everything. I value and appreciate you so much more than I ever told you," I whispered like we were in a room full of people and I only wanted her to hear me.

Grabbing her ring off her finger and her necklace and slipping them into my pocket, I walked around her room gathering her clothes and everything else she had here. Once I had everything, I made my way to the door and let the doctors know that they could take her.

I walked all the way from Jefferson Hospital back to West Philly. My mind was all over the place. There was always the thought of if my re-up money was messed up, how I would put it back, and my aunt always had me. As much as she didn't want me out on them blocks, Aunt Monica didn't want to see me hurt more. Manny always looked out too. We smoked so much weed just because we ain't have shit else to do. Unlike me, Manny ain't have to hustle, he just did for the simple fact that he loved the rush of it.

Manny came from some money. His parents were not filthy rich, yet they were hood rich. They had enough money to move out the hood and be comfortable and go and do as they pleased. That was how I wanted to be, not rich but not worried either.

I made it back to the house and went in to grab some water. My mouth was dry as hell, and sweat dripped down my face from the long walk. All I wanted to do was smoke and make some money. I had about five hundred dollars to my name, and seven hundred for my re-up money. Instead of grabbing again before I ran out like I usually did, I took all the money I had and went to my cousin's room. Knocking on the door, I waited for someone to answer. It took a while, but Trish, my cousin's girlfriend, finally opened the door. She had tears falling from underneath her glasses and her cheeks were a bright shade of red.

Trish ran her hands through her curly hair before pulling me into a hug.

"Hey, he's in there, but he's not talking. He has been calling his bank to see if he can get a loan, or anything. I've offered my help, but all I have is a two thousand. He's spent all he had on her chemo," She spoke.

Trish was about five foot five and Dominican. Her loyalty to my cousin was what stood out the most to me about her. She was a complete nerd just like him and they matched down to the matching glasses.

"Cool, all I have is about twelve hundred, and I'm willing to give it all to him," I told her honestly.

"So, we at a good start. She said she wanted to be cremated, because Ma started to look different and she wanted people to remember her for who she was, not what cancer made her look like. It will be about five thousand for the viewing and cremation all together. We close, we must get started on everything now. Is there anything you want to do? Mikey feels as though you should have as much input as he does." She wiped away a lone tear that fell from her eyes.

"Umm, I don't know. I want to help, but I don't know shit about none of this. I'm gone go in there and talk to him," I said, walking by her.

Mikey was sitting on his bed with his elbows resting on his knees and his head in his hands. I could hear him sobbing the closer I got to him.

"Cuz, look, we gone figure this shit out, man. I got some bread for you." I took the money wrapped in rubber bands out my pocket and placed it on the table. It wasn't a lot, but it was all I had. Shit, something was better than nothing.

"I'm about to go hit the blocks and hit them hard. I will have the rest of the money before the time you need it by, That's my word. We in this together. Don't feel alone, you got Trish and me. Keep your head up, she fought for as long as she could. You know Auntie been tired, but she held on for us. We got to make her prouder than we ever did now. This when it's gone count, we got to show the world that Monica raised us right, you feel me?" I rubbed his back, trying to comfort him.

"I hear you, man," he hiccupped.

I grabbed her ring and necklace and held them out to him. Our grandma, who had died when we were just kids, had given them to her and she never took them off. From what I heard, the jewelry that my mom had was long gone. She had sold it to the highest bidder to get high. Mikey grabbed the ring and left the necklace in my hand.

"You deserve to keep something of hers too, she was both our mom. Bro, honestly, I feel lost and don't even know where to start. I get a child is supposed to bury their parent, but I can't even do that. Once this is done and we get some stable income That's extra, I want us to go and get life insurance just in case. You know if anything happens to me, I want you to be okay. We need to do shit the right way while we are young and healthy." Mikey looked at me with bloodshot red eyes.

Nodding my head, I stood up and stuffed the necklace back into my pocket. Mikey stood and pulled me into a hug. He whispered in my ear that it was okay for me to cry. Pulling away from him, I walked out and headed downstairs. My aunt had a wall full of pictures of our family. I stared at the picture of the man and woman who were supposed to raise me, smiling next to me like they had just won a prize. That man and I had the same mocha complexion, the same full lips, light-brown slanted eyes. Seeing him made me realize where I got the good hair from and deep waves that came naturally. However, that was all I had gotten from him. Looking at myself in the mirror, I blinked away the tears that threatened to spill. Crying wasn't gone fix shit, I learned that a long time ago. I also learned from phone conversations with my so-called dad that men didn't cry, we held our head up and got shit right. Crying was for the weak, and that was the one piece of advice I took from him.

Walking onto the block, I kicked the trash can over. I knew I was going to have to do something to come up with re-up money, and fast. The sounds from the trash can flying into a car had a few heads snap my way.

"Yo, watch that shit. You just got trash all over my car," some nigga said as he stepped down off the steps.

"It look like I give a fuck where that trash went? You coming down here like your ass gone do something about it," I snapped.

This man didn't know the anger I was feeling. On a regular day, I would still knock his ass out for talking to me just because. Today, I was feeling like fuck the world and anybody could die, including me. So, when his ass hit the last step, I swung and put his ass to sleep.

"Fuck y'all looking at? Y'all can come get some this shit too!" I yelled at his peoples as I went to make my way up the steps. They all started reaching, but I ain't give not one single fuck. If it was my time to go, then I would welcome that shit with open arms.

"Ain't none of that 'bout to happen." I heard a gun cock and knew it was my nigga, Manny.

He snatched my ass back down the steps and pulled me away. Once we were up the block, he placed his gun in his pants and looked at me.

"Fuck is wrong with you? Nigga, that was Big O you just knocked the fuck out." He pushed me, and I knocked his arms down.

"Fuck Big O, he wants to see me when he wakes up, I'm gone be right here on this corner making money. My damn aunt needs to be buried, and I ain't in a position to do that. She gave me everything she could until her dying day, and the moment she needs me, I can't come through for her. I'm on this fucking block every day, and these little ass nick and dime bags ain't getting me nowhere, bro," I barked as I knocked some other shit over.

"Man, calm down, you know I got you. Look, I just grabbed, and I know you ain't gone let me just help you out. Take this pack and knock it off. Whatever you make, you can keep," he said, handing me a Ziploc bag of weed and a bundle of crack.

"Woah, when we get that white girl in?" I questioned.

"Earlier, I grabbed it for both of us to see what we can do, then we can see if this the route we want to take. Auntie needs the funds, though, and I know you gave ya whole stash up, so use this all to get you back to where you need to be. You my boy, we gone rock until the wheels fall off, but I don't need your ass out here starting no unwanted beef. I love you, bro, we family. Ain't shit in this world besides my bitch we can't share," Manny said.

I nodded my head and gave my boy snaps. He didn't know how much he just helped me out. Manny took a load off me and didn't even know it. Instead of keeping the conversation going, I hit the block, and hard. I didn't leave until I had everything off me, and enough to send my aunt home the right way. The rest of the money, I gave to Manny so he could grab more work. I was going to get it by any means, and if it meant no sleep and missing meals, then so be it.

3

MANNY

"And no one else can do what you have done for me. You will always be, you will always be the girl in my life. Mama, Mama, you know I love you," I had sung to my mom as we danced around the living room.

We did this every day. I went to her house for breakfast or dinner, and we danced around the house. There wasn't a lady in the world that I loved more than my mama. She was everything to me, my whole heart. I held on to my mom's small five-foot-two frame. My mom and dad had been married since they were eighteen.

"You're the perfect mixture of your daddy and me. You my world, Emmanuel, which is why when you hit these streets, you and Za need to be more careful. You know he hot headed and that shit with Monica only gone make him worse. You make sure you keep him levelheaded, 'cause that's my boy too, and you know your dad would flip if something happened to him." My mom smiled before pulling away to check on her pot roast.

My dad and I were close as hell. Even though Za wasn't blood related, my parents treated him like one of their own. Pops and my mom were teenage parents, and I was the spitting image of Maurice Taylor. We shared the same butter-pecan-colored skin, the same muscular build without even being in the gym, as well as the same deep waves and light-brown eyes that had bitches stuck for days. My dad was always considered a pretty boy, and my mom loved that shit. She swore up and down she had the finest man in the world, and him giving her a son that looked just like him only made her that much more hype. You couldn't tell my parents shit about me, and I felt the same way about them. My dad was the realest man in the world to me and nothing or no one could taint his image, and that was the way it would stay.

My phone rang and I quickly ignored it; no bitch could have my time when I was with my mom. It was all about her. Now that I was eighteen, I had moved into my own apartment. College was at one point a goal for me but when my accident happened, it was a dream that was shattered.

Laying my phone down, I went up to my old room and rolled up. While smoking, I thought about how close my dad and I really were and how my life with him went from great to just living. The one thing I wanted to do the most was taken away from me at an incredibly young age. I remember the shit like it was yesterday, and no money in the world could make me as happy as basketball used to. I was only a kid, thirteen to be exact, and about to go to high school and take basketball to a whole new level. My dad and mom had me training for years for these moments. It all changed one day hanging with my dad and his friends, which ended in a shootout and resulted in me being shot in the back.

"Son, you gone come with me today. We gone go to the courts and see your god dad," my dad said as he finished cutting my hair.

"Okay, Pops, you think you can help me work on my crossovers a little more? I want to be breaking people's ankles at the games."

"I got you, kid, now let's get your shirt on."

He dusted off my white beater, then I put my Lakers jersey on. My dad stood me in the mirror and made me look at myself. He waited for me to say what he taught me to say every day when I looked at myself in the mirror.

"I'm gone be the best because I will be at my best as long as I do my best. Keep your head up, King, because one day my queen will need a man. I'm going to be a man and a great one, I will lead with confidence and only walk away from a challenge if I need to because of circumstances and needing to make the right decision," I said before looking over into my dad's smiling face.

He dapped me up and we went outside. Time with my dad was my favorite time. I climbed in the front seat, and we drove through the city until we reached his old block. In the center of it was a basketball court with a bunch of kids already on it. As soon as I saw it, a wider smile graced my face, and I was ready to hop out and dunk on a few people.

"Come on, kid, you know the rules. Don't walk off, let me know if you going to the store, watch ya body. Keep ya eyes on everything going on, even when you are balling. And most importantly, win every game and take these lil' niggas' bread." My dad dapped me up, kissed my forehead, and sent me on my way. I all but ran over to the courts.

"Yo, Manny here. I call him, we 'bouta take all y'all bread, so get them fives out now," Sincere called.

I nodded my head and quickly joined his team. Sincere and I balled together in the summer at camp and every time I got to come around. We were the dynamic duo on the courts, and nobody was seeing us. Sincere and I took so much money from these people, my dad usually didn't have to give me lunch money. Just as we picked teams, I heard a bunch of yelling.

"Damn, we ain't even get the game going," I huffed and looked over to where the yelling was coming from. I saw my dad's best friend, Elijah, arguing with a guy.

Knowing Elijah, I knew that three things could happen. Either the guy could walk away, he would get knocked out, then there was the worst of them all: Elijah would kill him. He wouldn't do it now because of all the kids and females out, but sooner or later, this man would be on breaking news.

"Man, fuck that, them niggas be arguing all the time. I'm trying to play," Juice, one of the boys, said as he dribbled the ball.

"And you gone lose your money. Let's just see how this plays out first.

I'd rather cool and know what's going on than be over here playing and we end up getting hurt," I stated, moving near the tree and standing behind it for cover.

I scanned the area for my dad and saw him walking down the street with one of the local crackheads, probably selling him some shit. I kept my eyes on him and watched as he played it off like he wasn't aware of what was going on with Elijah. My dad loved for people to think they could catch him sleeping, and then he would surprise they asses. Back in the day, Logan won around fifty medals for boxing, so his hands were lethal. He also wasn't afraid to body a nigga and come home to his family like nothing happened.

"You think I'm a bitch or something?" I heard an unfamiliar voice say.

I looked at the car and took off running towards it, not really caring about playing ball anymore but being able to duck for safety. Just as I made it to the car, I heard Elijah's laugh.

"Fuck you reaching for?" my dad's voice boomed, and I was glad in that moment I had gotten low.

Nothing else was said, but a lot of shots rang out. I could hear my dad calling for me, so I peeked my head from behind the car and called him.

"Dad, I'm right here," I spoke.

My dad turned towards me and hauled ass my way. He wrapped his arms around me, making sure I was okay as the shots kept going.

"Listen, I'm hit. I need you to reach in my pocket and call your mom," my dad said as he placed his gun on the ground.

I did what he said and told my mom. She was yelling for our location while I was watching my dad's face frown from pain.

"Keep talking to her," he spoke.

I finally was able to get out where we were. The sounds of the shots stopped, and my dad told me to stay down. No cop sirens were heard yet, and I did what I thought was best to do. I stood up after grabbing my dad's gun and wiping it off. I handed it to one of the guys he always was around, just as the same guy who was arguing with Elijah raised his gun and fired off two shots. I felt the stinging before I knew what was going on. Four more shots were let off as my body fell to the ground.

"Manny," I could hear my dad calling me, but I couldn't respond.

Opening and closing my mouth, it slowly became hard and painful for me to breathe. I closed my eyes just as my mom's screams filled the air.

"Boy, what the fuck is you doing in here? You ain't hear me calling your ass? I should smack the shit out of you." My mom's voice brought me out of my thoughts.

"Why you always so loud? You good, Ma? What's up?" I questioned her.

"Yeah, I'm okay, I was trying to tell you the damn food done. Instead of answering me, your ass up in my house smoking and ain't bring me none, but don't want my ass going out there to buy none. Emmanuel, why you have that look on your face? Be honest with me, too, is your dad still being in jail bothering you? 'Cause your ass too old for that now. You understand he will be home sooner or later, ain't no snitching in us, so we gone bite that time if we have to. My husband is a stand-up man and he did his time with no worries. Shit almost over and we will be back together as a family again," my mom rambled as she went through my top drawer, grabbing my stash of weed.

"One day, you gone go through my stuff and find something you ain't looking for, and it ain't that." I frowned.

"Emmanuel, since it's not that, I'm gone need you to stop thinking about that shooting. It happened and it was years ago, we can't change it, and no, you didn't get to play basketball like you dreamed of, but you're well off. Even though you got accident money, you still not hurting, baby. You do right by that money you got, and it'll do right by you," she said, referring to the money I got from a car accident a few years back while on the bus. An eighteen-wheeler ran right into the back of the bus. It wasn't hard enough to where it killed anyone, but my ass flew with the backseat and got stuck between chairs. Which resulted in me breaking a few ribs and my leg. In the end, I was up a couple hundred thousand and the pain I had to go through was well worth it.

"Just because I have money don't mean I'm happy, all I

wanted to do was ball. That was my dream. I ain't have shit else planned, no back-up job, nothing else would make me as happy as winning a game on the court. I be feeling lost, Ma, like on some real shit. I just want to feel like I belong somewhere."

"Listen, one thing was taken out of your life to steer you in the direction of something else. Basketball just wasn't your calling; you will find something. What else is it you like to do? Sit and think about it, plan it out. Son, I want you to be happy more than anything. I love you, and thank you for my weed." My mom kissed my forehead and left me with something to think about.

I would find something that I liked to do or wanted to do, and I would give it my all and let nothing stop me.

❧ 4 ❧

JUSTINE

Walking into my dorm, I kicked the bed and cursed loudly from the pain that shot through my big toe up my leg. Ms. Maria had come and let me know that I was going to be getting a new roommate soon, and I didn't like it. I loved being by myself. These bitches in this place were bound to have my ass in the juvenile detention center from trying me, and a new roommate was probably bound to do just that.

I learned not to give a damn about people early on in life. I had been in here since I was thirteen and now at seventeen, friends were the least of my worries.

My mother was taken from me the day after she gave birth to me. The only memories of her I had was a picture of me laying on her chest that my father had taken. He told me that she had gotten a bad infection, which killed her. My dad raised me up until I was thirteen, then he began to look at me different and tell me how much I reminded him of my mother. The more my looks matured, the more he would stay away from me. I went from being my dad's entire world to a person he couldn't look at for more than five minutes. My mom and I both were what people like to call black as hell, and I heard it a whole lot growing up too. Everyone would tease me and call me midnight. I had thick hair that often looked nappy and was always told I needed a perm instead of keeping my hair in a big puff ball. Everything about me was dark, my eyes, lips, and hair. My teeth were a bright white, and I had a small gap in between my two front teeth, which also got me teased.

Justin, my dad, said one day he couldn't take it anymore and dropped me off at school and never came back to get me. I could remember the day like it happened yesterday. I waited for hours before walking home, only for the locks to be changed and no one answered the door. There was no way I would forget how I banged on that door for hours and hours with no answer. Once my arm hurt, I began to kick it, leaving a dent in the door. My phone was dead, and I didn't have any friends that I trusted whose place I could go to. Sitting down on the steps, I waited until night turned into morning. The next day, I didn't go to school, fearing I would miss him. Days turned into weeks, with no sight of my dad and no one coming in or out the house. My sitting went from the front steps to the back because I didn't want anyone to see me. The back porch became my bedroom. I would go to school for breakfast and lunch then leave, saving the lunch for the night so I could have dinner. Eventually, my school called DHS on me, and they took me straight from school.

When they couldn't reach anyone in my family, they shipped me to a foster home, where I was beaten and raped by my foster mother and her boyfriend. That's a story y'all can't get, because no therapy would ever allow me to relive that one for anybody.

Sitting on my bed, I had to laugh when this girl walked in. She looked like life had beat her, and bad. That look was all too familiar. Now, I could have spoken to her, but when she walked in, she ain't speak and had her head hanging down. I'd never been one to start a conversation, and I wasn't about to start. I did hope that whatever had her feeling like she was, would go away. I ain't wish bad on nobody, especially not when the cards you were dealt landed you here.

"Denver, this is your roommate, Justine. Justine, Denver," Ms. Maria introduced us.

Denver looked at me and gave me a small wave, which I returned. She pushed her small bin against the wall and plopped down on her bed, letting out a sigh.

Denver was beautiful, even with the frown that was plastered on her face. She was the kind of girl I used to wish I looked like; however, I knew now that my dark skin was just as beautiful as her light skin. She reminded me of Steve Harvey's daughter, Lori, or whatever her name was. While people always used to call me a black ass version of Gabriel Union. I stood up and walked over to her.

"Hey, look, whatever it is can't be that bad, it will get better." I tried to be nice since we had to basically live with each other.

"It can't be that bad? Bitch, my baby just got taken away from me. Fuck you mean? You should have just kept your ass over there and kept ya damn mouth shut," she snapped at me.

I had to take a step back and look at her. She had me fucked up when I was just trying to be nice.

"You know what, fuck you, I was trying to be nice. Cry ya life away and see if that shit helps you. You're 'bout twelve with a fucking baby. God don't make no mistakes, so you keep talking to me like that and see if he makes a mistake when I knock your young ass the fuck out," I snapped back. That was why I said fuck people now.

"Twelve? Just because I'm small don't mean I'm no little ass girl. I'm sixteen, and you ain't gone knock shit out. When you go sit back in that corner looking crazy as hell like you was when I came in here, you better ask that same God you referring to about me. Last muthafucka that tried me got they shit handed to them." She stood up off her bed like she was ready to fight.

I smirked at her then walked off. Had I not gotten written up already this week, I would have taken her up on her offer. A job was something I wanted more than anything to get my own money. The moment I turned eighteen, I planned on leaving this place, but I couldn't do it empty handed. I knew fighting wouldn't help me. The workers here already thought I was a problem and would have sworn up and down I started this one.

"You got it, baby girl. I got too much I'm trying to do to get up out of here. Keep it up, though, and promise you won't tell, and I'll give you exactly what that attitude is asking for." I sat on my bed, and this bitch had the nerve to stomp over towards me.

"Get the fuck up and let's go. Either you stand up now or I'm gone punch you in your shit while you're sitting down," she snarled, and I laughed. This girl was so tiny I could blow and sit her ass down.

She stood there for a second before she swung, hitting me in the jaw. I had to run my tongue across the top of my mouth to see if I tasted blood, while standing up. She grabbed my hair and kept swinging. Of course, I locked on to hers and swung back.

"You thought shit was sweet, huh?" she said while pushing her body forward, causing us to fall on the bed with her on top of me. In that moment, she had the upper hand. This little ass girl placed her knees on my arms and punched me in the face multiple times. Using my upper body, I pushed her up and turned, landing us on the floor with a big thud. This time I was on top, and I delivered what I could to her face. We went at it until we were tired, both of us were huffing and puffing while holding on to each other's hair.

"Bitch, if I let you go, you bet not swing on me. I'm tired and ain't trying to fight no more," she said through breaths.

"You bet not swing on me either," I growled, out of breath myself.

We both let each other go and backed up, preparing ourselves for the other to swing. Laughing at each other when we didn't, and standing there waiting.

"Fuck it, I'm Denver, nice to meet yo' ass." She laughed while licking the blood from her lip.

I wiped the blood from my nose on my shirt before introducing myself. I was impressed. In all my years of being in this place, wasn't none of these bitches' hands nice enough to fuck with me, yet this small ass girl gave me a run for my money.

"My bad for the attitude, I just dealt with a lot today. My mom basically ain't even give a fuck that the people were coming to get me. They took my baby from me, and I'm angry with the world. I never been away from her for this long. I ain't even a fighter, I will fight, but I don't like to. I don't bother nobody. You were a rare case of just caught the anger I was feeling from the situation. Girl, my ass is lost, and don't know if I will ever find myself. I apologize for coming at you like that when you were just being nice to me," she admitted as tears rolled down her eyes.

"You are good, we are good. Shit happens, and I have had my days. My dad was like that. Well, his ass just up and left me. As far as my mom, she died giving birth to me, so I basically feel like ain't nobody for me. Hell, everybody left me to sleep on the back porch like I wasn't a child," I said, opening some shit I hated to talk about.

Denver waved her hands like she wanted me to continue, but that was it. I was currently in therapy for this exact same reason. Sharing my life story was something I didn't want to do, nor did I do. The more her body shuddered from her cries, the more I wanted to go over there and hug her. Shit, I always felt numb. I wanted to express to her that things would happen how they were supposed to. That was something I told myself when I began to feel down, yet, I ain't want to risk getting punched in the face again. Sitting on my bed, I stared blankly at the beige-colored wall. Wasn't nothing for me to do to help her. Listening to her sniffles made a few tears of my own fall. She reminded me of myself when I first got here. I felt lost, helpless, sad, confused, anger, disappointment, betrayal, pain, and most of all, broken. The mixture of those feelings caused me to be who I am today.

Everyone around me thought I was just this mean person, when deep down I wasn't. I kept my guard up because I refused to be left alone and hurt again. To add to it, I had trouble reading, like bad. My father couldn't read, and he never bothered to teach me. I was damn near grown reading on a second-grade level, and that was something I was constantly teased about, and the teachers here lived by the "I don't care if you learn or not, I'm still gone get my check."

I really felt like I never really had a chance at succeeding in life, which was why I wanted to badly. Every way I looked at it, I was fucked. Even when I tried my hardest, failure still met me like it was waiting for me at the door. I constantly felt like I survived an abortion and wasn't really meant to be here. Death had to be easy, because life was hard.

❦ 5 ❧

DENVER

I woke up with a headache. It had been three months since I had been taken away from my baby and I had not seen her since. My baby was eight months today and my nerves were a wreck. I had completed every class they made me take over the time. Getting my baby back had become my focus. I knew that once I turned eighteen, if I was still here, they would help me get myself an apartment and a job. So far, I hadn't had any fights but the one with Justine. She and I became really close after that. We helped each other a whole lot, and I now called her my best friend.

"Girl, this the day you been waiting for. I wish I could come with you to meet my niece." Justine smiled as I fixed my bun in the small mirror.

"I know, I'm going down now. I'll get some pictures on my phone." Holding up my flip phone, I ran out of the room and down to the visiting room.

Once I was inside, I waited all of ten minutes before an older lady walked in with my baby. She came over and sat down. I reached for Dakota and when she didn't reach out for me back, my heart broke.

"Hey, Kota, girl, Mommy missed you." I grabbed her anyway and held her close to me.

For the first five minutes I held her and cried while the lady just sat there and stared at us. Kissing all over her face and tickling the spot that usually would have my baby smiling made her whine.

"Aww, my baby, what's wrong?" I asked like Dakota could answer me.

Turning my attention to this newly found aunt, my questions began.

"Hey, I'm Denver. I have not ever got to meet you because of whatever reason, and I don't care too much about that. What I do care about is why Dakota is behaving so different. Usually, she is a happy baby. She is always smiling, cooing, and everything else. Is everything okay, has she been like this for a while? How's her doctor's appointments and all those things been? You think I could go with you to one? They didn't say I couldn't, so it is not breaking any rules. Where is your husband? I would like to meet him. How is he with Kota? Is she around anyone else?"

Ms. Lady looked at me and rolled her eyes before placing a fake smile on her face.

"Dakota is fine, she's just a baby. As for my husband, he couldn't make it. He had other things to do. I don't want you at her appointments and honestly, I came here because I wanted to tell you that a visit once a week like you're requesting is a whole lot for me as far as traveling. This is about an hour ride, and I'm not willing to do it every week. We can agree on twice a month, I can do that," she said.

"Any way I can see her is fine with me, ma'am, and I want to thank you for taking her. I appreciate it, and as soon as I'm able to get her, I will." Sensing that the lady ain't have too much to say to me, I spent my time focusing on my baby.

The entire time, Dakota smiled about five times in total. Yes, I counted. Towards the end, she started smiling more. When it was time to hand her back, my heart broke in a way I thought it couldn't anymore.

"Thank you for allowing me to see her. I really appreciate everything you have done for her thus far."

"You're welcome," she said before snatching my baby out of my harms and walking out.

I wanted to say something about the way she grabbed her but decided against it. Wasn't no way I was going to fuck up my chances on seeing my baby again. I still didn't even know the lady's name and would be asking my workers about that and how carefully they were really watching my baby with that family. Just as I got up to go tell Justine about my day, the devil herself walked in looking good as ever, turning all the heads in the room. One thing about Treasure was she demanded attention anywhere she went, and she got it.

I watched as she strutted across the room. Just like my baby and I shared the same looks, we got it from her. Treasure's makeup was done flawless, and the weave in her head was just as good. Over the years, I developed her body type. We stood at the same five-foot height, and she was thirty-four, with the same small waist and a body that women would go out their way to pay for. Even with her in baggy sweatpants and a fitted shirt, you could make out her body. With her coffee in her hand and a smile on her face, she sat in front of me.

"What's good, look alike. Heard you wanted to speak with me," she said, sitting her drink down.

"I did, and you finally found time to talk. Ma, you know what I wanted you here for," I expressed.

You would think after months of not seeing her only child she would embrace me, and though I kept a hard exterior on the inside, I was dying for her to pull me into a hug, tell me she was doing better to get me out, and for once in my life that she loved me.

"Girl, leave that man where he at. I want to say he dead but shit, I don't know. Why you even care where he's at? You good.

You don't look like you're doing so bad, and I just seen Dakota when I was leaving out. Look, boo, my life is going fine. I been taking these classes and doing shit to get y'all back together. On the real, I'm trying to do this for you because it's the least I can do. I'm just doing it on my own time, which is taking it slow, so when you turn eighteen, they can get you ya own shit and up out of mine. I ain't want no damn kids. You stopped me from enjoying my teenage years and I ain't about to let you stop my adult ones."

"Treasure, you wild for that. You know I ain't ask for you to fuck and make me, you did that, and the fact you don't even want to tell me information to get me out of your hair and help you live your best life is fucked up." Treasure taught me at a young age to express myself and not hold back, even with her. Often, I found myself holding back anyway. It didn't matter how she felt about me, she was still my parent, and as much as she raised me to be a disrespectful child, it just wasn't in me to be that.

"Oh, and the bitch finally found a voice after how long? Let me explain this to you, I'm gone live mine, which you already know. I ain't give a fuck about you, so what makes you think I'ma give a single fuck about your kid? You need my help, hoe, not the other way around. Now you want to find ya daddy and his family, start searching, 'cause I ain't got shit for you." She smirked, and I snapped.

Standing up, I slapped the shit out of Treasure, knocking her glasses off top her head. Before the security could get to us, Treasure had a lock on my hair and we both swung wildly.

"I'm fucking hate you, bitch. I swear to God this is all your fault. You never take blame for shit you do!" I screamed as I pounded on the back of her head as hard as I could. I was biting my lip so hard I knew I would leave a mark.

"Denver, let go of my hair. I'm not gone swing back on you no more," Treasure said, sounding defeated.

Instead of letting go, I let out all my anger towards her and even held on as the security tried prying my hands from her hair. Treasure had long ago stopped fighting me back, yet that didn't stop me. I hated her, and with every punch I was sure to let her know. When we were finally pulled apart, I was breathing hard and crying.

"I guess I see how you feel now. That's cool, though, I do love you, girl, but fuck you, and I mean that. You want answers, yo' daddy name Maurice, he married, and his mother's name is Ann, they last name is Taylor. That's all I got for you. Denver, let me tell you this, I refrained from beating your ass 'cause you right, all this shit is my fault. Let that be your last time swinging on me, though, because the next time, I'm swinging back. And we both know you ain't messing with me on that level. Don't worry about me doing shit to get your disrespectful ass back, because I don't want shit to do with you. Good riddance, bitch!" Treasure screamed before she made her exit.

Nothing she said bothered me. All that even mattered was she gave me a name to my father and grandmother, and I had somewhere to look. Ms. Maria made her way to me with a sad expression on her face. Even though I had just fought with my mom, I was happy, my daughter was growing, and we spent time together, and I was one step closer to possibly getting some help and us back together. Ms. Maria was talking to me while I was silently repeating the names in my head, so they were not forgotten.

"Do you hear me right now?" Ms. Maria snapped her fingers in my face.

"No, my bad. Look, please make sure you have somebody go check on my baby. Like thoroughly, something was up with her. She wasn't the same baby and her mood was different. I can't quite put my finger on what's wrong, but I know my baby. She didn't look well, and she didn't too much like the lady, who by the way name I still don't even know. We must do something about all of this. I feel since my child is with these people, I should know more and be in contact more. Oh, and could you please have my DHS worker investigate a Maurice and Ann Taylor? Treasure said they were my dad and grandma."

"Okay, we can get into that. You can't be fighting, Denver, your mom at that. No matter what she said, you must learn to control yourself. All you gone do is make it harder on yourself to get that beautiful baby back. You are far too pretty and smart to be doing that. You've been here and have steered clear of trouble. You've done all you had to, to get your child back, and now you have more information, making you a step closer. Don't fuck it all up over her," she spoke low so that only I could hear her.

Nodding my head, I made sure to ask her again to have them do a random pop up and check on my baby and that family. They could say what they wanted, but I didn't see love or nothing caring radiating off that lady that walked out with my heart in human form. I walked off and went back into my room. Justine was laying on her bed looking at a dictionary. She had told me about her reading problem, so we stole the book from the store and had been working on her learning words every day. I climbed on her bed and told her all about what had just went down.

"She's right, unlike the rest of us, you got somebody that's waiting on you. Make her proud, take these moments away from her, and get back in school, get your shit right, so when you have her back, can't nobody tell you shit or do shit. Show them you ain't gone fail. That's what everybody waiting on, sis. Baby girl gone be okay, it was probably because she hadn't seen you in a while. I don't want to tell you, you right or wrong. Stand on what you believe and press the issue until they do what you asked them. Listen, we gone make it if nothing else we do in this world. We gone become something. Just keep holding that head up high," Justine said. I heard everything she said, but for some reason, all I cared about was them going out unannounced and making sure no harm was coming my child's way.

❧ 6 ❧

MANNY

Placing my hand on Za's back, I walked him out of the funeral home and to one of the cars. My boy was breaking down bad for Auntie, and I had shed a few tears myself. She was good to all of us. Za was showing a different side of him that nobody wanted to see. He was a firm believer that he had a cold heart and held no emotions; however, he wasn't showing that. Right before entering the cars, I grabbed him by his shoulders and forced him to look at me.

"Bro, we got to turn up from here. I'm not gone let you go downhill. Whatever you need, you know I got you. Put that pride shit to the side and speak up. You know whatever I got, you got. I know how you get with shit like this, so if you want to pay me back for whatever you need, you can, but here is the payback I want and it is the only form, take off. Become who you need to become successful." We locked eyes and he nodded.

Pulling his weed from behind his ear, he sparked it up and took a long pull while gazing at the funeral home. Silent tears spilled from his eyes, and I felt fucked up seeing my boy like this. His cousin left before the whole service was over. He broke down the moment they closed that casket and ain't been back since.

"Arghhhh!" I heard Zamir yell, and I placed my hand back on his shoulder. The way his tears were falling had me dropping a few of my own. Sitting there quietly, I let him get it all out. I knew his breakdown would come, I just didn't know when. My mom came over to him and wrapped her arms around him. He bent down and cried into her shoulder, his body trembling while she rubbed his back.

"Ma, this shit hurt different. What am I 'pose to do now? I miss her so much and it ain't even been long. I feel like she been gone so much longer than she has been. Man, every night I stay up smoking outside her room door in hopes of her calling my name and telling me take that shit to my room," he cried out.

"Let it out, baby," was all my mom said.

My mom slowly rocked him back and forth while talking to him. A group of people walked over to give their condolences and kept going. Zamir didn't want to attend the repast and whatever he wanted to do, I was rocking with him. Once he pulled away from my mom, he used his shirt to wipe his face and we jumped in my car. We headed straight to the trap house that we called the bando, because I knew this would take his mind off things. I parked the car and went to get out, but Za's hand touching me halted my movements.

"What's good, bro? I figured this spot would ease ya mind a little," I confessed.

"Shit, it would if I had the bread to make moves. All my shit went to Auntie, every penny I had. I'm gone have to hit a few licks again to get back in position. Even though I was flipping small shit, it was enough to make sure I wasn't dead broke," he admitted.

Reaching in my middle console, I grabbed the envelope I kept there for emergency money. It was only about four thousand, small change to me, but I knew to Zamir it would be a lot. Only thing was, I was hoping he took it without much of a fuss, because Za didn't like handouts. I tried to toss it in his hand, yet he snatched his hand away like hot grease spilled on him. I looked at him before laughing, while he sat there with a scowl on his face.

"Bro, fuck is that? You could have given me five hundred. That's some shit I could pay back in about two weeks tops. That jawn thick as fuck, and I know it's more than that," Za snapped at me.

"It's four racks, you should be good for a minute. I told you how you could pay me back, but your ass doesn't listen. You in here jumping around like ya ass itch," I shot back.

"Fuck you, bitch boy, I ain't taking that shit no way. I heard what you said, but fuck that got to do with on my end? You helped me enough when you helped with Auntie shit, bro. I can't keep taking from you. You done bought me shoes, hell even gave me a pair off your feet. Hooked me up with clothes, covered me in a lot of situations, bro. You have done enough; it is nothing for me to go out here and take a nigga shit. I'd rather that than to keep taking from you," he barked.

Leaving the envelope with him, I jumped out the car and made my way inside the house. Just like always, fiends were everywhere. I headed straight to the basement and to Kilo to grab some work. I watched as he bagged and weighed crack while smoking weed. Kilo looked up at me and nodded, I returned the head nod.

"What's good, lil' nigga, what you are grabbing?" he asked before trying to pass me his blunt. I quickly declined. That man had a bunch of crack residue on his fingers, and even though I loved weed, I ain't love it that much.

"I need a pound," I said, eyeing the work he was cutting up. I swore up and down I wouldn't touch that shit, but the money was way faster than this little weed money.

"We'll grab you some of this work since you keep looking at it. I know for a fact if you can't get it off your hands your boy can. That nigga got potential to be the fucking plug the way he plays them blocks," Kilo boasted on Za, and he was right. Za was a hustler at heart. He could sell anything, and that's what made all the drug dealers want to put him on. My boy wasn't with working for nobody and with his work ethic, I wouldn't want to either.

Just as I tossed the money on the table, Za came busting through the damn door like the police. Kilo grabbed his gun and pointed it in his direction, which made me point mine in his. I didn't care how much pull Kilo had, I would pay any amount of money to protect my peoples and kill whoever didn't fall in line if it ever became us or them. When Kilo dropped his gun, I lowered mine and placed it back on my hip. Za's dumb ass was smirking like a kid in the candy store.

"Kilo, you got to stop raising your gun on me every time I come in here. I'm starting to think your ass wants to shoot me. I need some work, and I need green and that white girl. Don't try and front me no shit either. I don't even know how much the shit cost, so don't try and play me on no bullshit, 'cause next time it won't be the door I just bust, but yo' head too," Za threatened him.

"Man, one day I'm gone knock yo' ass out. You better be lucky you my boy god-son," Kilo shot back with a light chuckle.

Kilo and my pops ran together before my dad got knocked for drugs. They wanted him to snitch, but that shit fell on deaf ears. My dad took his time and was doing it with his head held high, which earned him a whole lot more respect on these streets.

"Come on, Kilo, you're 'bout ten years older than me, you know for sure you can't fuck with me. But anyway, for real, I got three stacks for you right now. I need a pound of weed and the rest that white girl," Za spoke, pulling the money from the envelope.

This nigga was damn near going all in. I swore he was gone at least take part of it and grab himself some shit; however, knowing him, he was about to bury himself in these streets so he didn't have to go home and face reality. Once we got our shit, we headed to the back room that only we went into. Kilo had let us have that room and only we had the key to it. To a person coming in it looked like a regular four-bedroom house with a fully finished basement. However, everything went on in this place. Placing my package on the bed, we pulled out the table and got right to work. For about an hour straight it was complete silence as we bagged up and sorted our shit out. Za ain't know shit about selling no crack, but I had faith in him. He sat there looking confused while trying to figure out how the shit worked.

"Bro, just go ask one of them niggas," I told him, and he frowned at me.

"If I fuck up, I fuck up, I ain't asking them niggas shit. Will not nobody out that bitch say I needed they help. I'ma learn on my own. I'm gone be hood rich, watch. A nigga down bad right now, but give me a year and watch. I'm not spending nor buying shit, ain't like I'm gone miss anything," he said as his phone rang.

By the way he smacked his teeth, I could tell it was one of his many bitches he dealt with. Za and I were considered hoes because we ran through females. I kept them around because I liked some of them, but my boy was the opposite. He hit and left them alone. The results of that were them stalking us both to get to him.

"I ain't even got time for no pussy. I'm on the block getting money. Unless the bitch handing over some bread, she can't get none of my time. I'm on a mission for real, bro." He laughed as he powered off his phone.

I sat there with him helping him bag up, and then we hit the block. Once we were on the steps we smoked and sold as much work as we could until I got tired. I knew Za ain't plan on leaving the block no time soon, so after making sure he had his strap, I got up and headed towards my car. I walked right into Daisy and sucked my teeth.

"So, this how I got to keep up with you? Misha told me she been with you and I ain't believe it, so you are messing with my so-called friend?" She pointed her finger in my face.

"Girl, if you don't move. Take that up with your girl. We ain't together and if she opened her legs to me, that's something y'all got to discuss. If she let me, I'm gone dig in them guts again too, 'cause it was good and gushy." I smirked.

The way her face balled up, I had to laugh. She was acting a fool and mad at me when her friend came to me, I just ain't turn it down. To me, I didn't owe anybody anything but dick. Trying to step around her without touching her, she moved back in my way.

I rubbed my temples as my frustrations grew. I didn't put my hands on females, and she was about to make me go against everything my mom and grandma had taught me.

"You not gone sit here and show off like you weren't just telling me sweet nothings and sleeping in my bed or having me over at ya grandma's house all the time." She pointed her red fingernail in my face.

I calmly removed her hand from my face and pulled open my car door. My anger grew when she slammed the door back closed. Taking my perfectly rolled chocolate Dutch from behind my ear, I lit it and blew the smoke in her face. Daisy hated smoke, so she quickly took a step back.

"What you want from me? Dick? I ain't giving it out today." I laughed at her.

"Fuck you, I hope your little dick falls off!" she screamed.

Again, I smirked before climbing in my car. I went to pull off and she kicked my car. Putting it in park, I jumped out and looked over my shit. Daisy had put a big dent in the side of my car, and her smile was quickly wiped off her face when I gripped her ass up and slammed her against the car.

"You want me to go against everything I was taught and knock ya ass out. On my grandmama, I'm ready to break ya shit," I barked at her.

"Boy, if you don't put her ass down, I'm gone bust your ass. And little miss lady, keep your damn feet and hands to yourself.

Your mammy ain't teach you that?" My grandma made her way down the street.

I quickly let Daisy go and backed away from her. Grandma Ann was all of four foot eleven inches and played no games. Back in the day, she ran with the best of them, and she swore she still had it. Just like always, she had her Louisville slugger bat in her hand with her old lady gown with the flowers on it. To me, my grandmother was beautiful. She had slight wrinkles on her face, and she kept her gray hair dyed black.

"Man, Grandma, the bitch—I mean girl kicked a dent in my car. I let her slide with a whole lot, but she just won't let me leave," I pleaded my case. Grandma was the only person who could ever make me fold and have me feeling like a kid just by her facial expressions.

"Fuck all that, why you ain't been by to see me in days? Your ass been around too, and y'all ain't even bother to tell me about Monica. How my baby Za doing? I know he hurt, he ain't even been by to get no food. I'm gone tell y'all this, you and Zamir need to come down the street and see me when y'all asses out here. It only takes a twenty-second walk and thirty minutes out y'all day, and you, girl, get your ass on. Don't ever let nobody have you out here making a fool of yourself," she said before storming off back down the street.

I looked over, and Za's dumb ass was hiding beside the bando, peeking out. Laughing, I got in my car, parked it, and went down the street to spend time with my second favorite lady.

❧ 7 ❧

JUSTINE

I looked at the word Denver held out in front of me and sighed. We had been locked away in this room for a while now, and I had only learned two words. I felt like I would never be able to read.

"Come on, it's P-A-R-T-Y, party," Denver spelled and sounded out the word for me.

I did it with her and smiled when I finally got it. Denver was taking her time and helping me when she didn't have to, and I appreciated her so much for it. The teachers here didn't even put this much effort out for us.

"That was the last one for today. Come on so we can go hit this dollar store up. I want to get my baby something. I'm supposed to have a visit with her this weekend, and I want to have something for her."

It wasn't too often I went out but when I did, I enjoyed the moments. Most people left to go to work or just to go hang out. Since I didn't really have anybody to go out in the world and see, I never really walked around. Digging around through my clothes, I pulled on a pair of tights and a hoodie. We headed out the door and walked the few blocks to the dollar store. Inside, we got as much as we could fit into our bags and pockets before heading back out. The cashier looked at me and shook his head as he stood on the wall smoking a cigarette.

"Aye, let me talk to you for a minute," he said, pulling at my arm.

"I'm too young," I said, trying to get away.

He nodded his head and smirked at me but let me continue my walk. I had to jog slightly to catch up to Denver. Her ass had basically left me back there so she could get away.

"Damn, bitch, you were just gone leave me?" I said, out of breath, when I made it to her.

She laughed and shrugged like she didn't care. We kept walking until we made it back and sat on the steps. I investigated the sky and thought about how my life would be if my dad had stayed or even where he was. My mind raced as I thought of if he even thought about me or if I was okay. Had he gone back to check on me, or did he just erase me out of his mind? I had so many questions for this man, and one day I was going to ask him. That would be my dying wish to ask this man these questions. My mind quickly drifted to what I would do when I left here. My eighteenth birthday was slowly approaching and I had nothing planned. The only thing that was guaranteed for me was that this place would be something behind me. I had done my time here, and while I was thankful for the help and Denver coming into my life, this place wasn't going to help me once it was time for me to go.

"Girl, what your ass thinking about? You so quiet. If your ass mad I kept walking, then ain't no need to be. If I would have gotten caught up with you it would have fucked up my chances on getting Dakota. Ain't nothing out there for me but her. I'm going to do everything I got to do for her, which is why I stay clear of the bullshit and the messy bitches," Denver said, staring a hole into Leslie.

Leslie was one of the many girls who hated us for no reason. She didn't even know us, but any chance she got, something slick was coming out of her mouth, especially when we had class. If they played popcorn, the bitch would send the shit my way every time, and instead of reading, my ass would just get up and walk out. One time she tried it and I popped her right in the mouth. You would think she left me alone after that, but she didn't. We both watched her as she climbed into an all-black Crown Vic that had tinted windows, and wondered who was inside. One thing I could say about Leslie was she stayed fresh and in the latest clothes. She was always out and in a man's car. It was safe to say she was tricking, and if that's how she got by and kept money in her pockets, then good for her. Hell, I almost wanted to do the same thing. It looked as if that life was treating her good, and my little hot virgin ass wanted a piece of it, and bad.

As the car pulled off, Leslie rolled the window down and stuck her middle finger out at us, which I quickly returned. Her ass wouldn't be doing all that shit if she wasn't in that car.

"You still ain't answer me, and I been asked you a question like four minutes ago. Ain't no way you that mad, and if you are, oh fucking well at this point," Denver snapped at me, and I had to laugh.

"Girl, calm ya coochie. I ain't mad at you, I get you got shit to lose. My ass can't just think? Shit, just like you be trying to figure your shit out, I am too. Ain't nothing out in that world for me right now that I know of. I got to make it for me, and without a clue where to start. I'm lost. I will be eighteen soon, and that's when I'm gone be gone. I been here long enough and even with no plans, I want to see what the world got in store for me," I admitted honestly.

"How about start with planning what you want to do? Where you want to be. I know I have been taking them classes because I want to finish school, get my high school diploma, and go off to college. Even if it's a community college, I want to go and graduate, get a degree, and take care of my daughter. I also want to get a job working somewhere just to grab us an apartment or something, you know. If all else fails, we can be roommates when we get out of here. We both can split the bills and rely on each other when we need to, just like in here. If you got me as a friend, we would figure shit out together. You not just gone be left here high and dry or out in the world to make a fool of yourself. I don't know how, but I know we gone be good, and that's all you got to see is the bigger picture. The one you want, and take steps every day to have that picture as your reality." Denver smiled.

"That shit sounds like a plan. When you become a motivational speaker?" I joked.

"Shit, I don't even know. It sounded good as hell, though, that's why I kept talking, surprised my own damn self. I had got this bag of weed we can smoke right fast, we just got to get a wrap." Denver held the bag of weed out, and it made my mouth water.

After hiding our stuff we had just taken in the bushes, we headed to the Chinese store on the corner. A few crack heads and drug dealers lingered around. Looking for someone who would be able to get us a chocolate Dutch, I spotted Kilo. Kilo was cool with everyone in the hood and was seeing a lot of money. If he dated young girls, I would surely give him my virginity without second thought just to live the life I knew he could provide me. Walking over to him, I put an extra twitch in my hips like it would matter. He was leaned against the car with a toothpick in his mouth. He had on an oversized white T-shirt and a Sixers jersey on with a pair of blue jeans. This man was drop dead gorgeous too, with his light bright ass. I would braid his hair any day too.

"Hey, could you go in there and get us a chocolate Dutch?" I asked him as I pulled the balled up two dollars out of my pockets.

He looked at my hand before he looked at my face. No longer was he smiling, the smile was quickly replaced with a deep scowl on his face.

"Nah, little girl, I can't help your ass, you jailbait. Better go ask one of them lil' niggas. You see all these muthafuckas and you have the nerve to come over here. You are not the fuck slick, little hot ass," he snapped.

I went to snap back but thought about it. Even with my life not being shit, I didn't want to lose it. Sucking up my pride and not letting my ego win, I turned to one of the younger guys and got him to do it. Denver was standing off to the side watching everything. When the guy came back and handed me my stuff, I took one last look at Kilo.

"Eighteen in a few months and watch me have his ass," I said loud enough for him to hear me.

He let out a deep chuckle. For him to be forty-something years old, he was so fine to me. I knew I wanted to lose myself to someone older because they knew how to love on you and do your body right. They were older with much more experience, and that's what I wanted and needed in my life. We headed over to the park and sat on the bleachers. While Denver rolled up, I sat there and looked at the boys play basketball. My favorite part was when they would jump, and they print would swing. My ass was in heat and wanted some more than a little. All I saw were girls and what they had going. I wasn't sure if I was simply curious or if seeing them naked made me horny as well. I often acted like Denver getting dressed in front of me didn't faze me, yet her body was something to look at. I always had to remind myself that she was my sister and not somebody to mess with; however, if she tried anything with me, I wouldn't stop her.

"Stop staring and grab the weed, or I can smoke by myself." Denver smiled, showing off her deep dimples.

"Them niggas got some nice-size dicks and I'm ready for somebody to come snatch this cherry," I replied, dancing in my seat. Grabbing the weed out her hand, I took a deep pull and held it in. Weed always made everything I felt go away. Shit numbed my feelings and everything going on in the world.

❧ 8 ❧

ZAMIR

Catch me any day you want, you could think I'ma play if you want
But the fact still remains if I got an AK, and you don't
Well then playa you gone
Don't get me wrong, there's some niggas want to kill me too
But they ain't saying 'bout shit because they very well know where I'm at
They could catch me in the booth right if it really like that

I bobbed my head to the beat and rapped T.I.'s song "Hurt" that played on the little radio in the corner. After clearing the small table, I pulled my hoodie off and sat it on the bed. I had been at the trap a week straight, only leaving to wash my ass. Grabbing the razor and glass plate I needed, I got to work. I knew I needed at least an hour to bag up. It would be the first of the month in a few hours, and I was gone beat the addicts outside. While everyone else was sleeping, I would be out making all the money. This had become my life. I slept about two to three hours a day. Each day I grew more tired, but nothing was stopping me from getting this money, not even sleep. When the clock hit twelve on the wall like Cinderella, I was up out that bitch and on the block.

"Za, let me get six of them, and here's the money I owed you from last week," Gene, one of the local crack heads, said.

I was glad he gave me my money, because I was on the verge of knocking his ass out. I slid what he wanted to him in his hand while watching the block for any cops. At the same time, he handed me my money and was gone. My phone rang, causing a sigh to leave my mouth. Kelly, a chick I had been fucking more than anybody else, kept calling me. Usually, I hit a bitch one time and left. We went by this saying find 'em, fuck 'em, flea 'em, and that's what I did. With Kelly, I may have stuck dick in her too many times. She was twenty-four with her own crib and working as a receptionist at a dental office. She was pretty, and the thing I liked most about her was she stayed about a half hour away from the hood. I would go to her house sometimes just to lay around, but it was never long enough for the girl to feel like I wanted anything more than to sling dick. When my phone rang again, I picked it up.

"I'm on the block, ma, you gone have to hit me later," I said before she could even speak.

"Baby, I miss you and I need some dick. I can come pick you up whenever you done if I'm still woke, and you can just keep my car and drop me off at work," she whispered.

The sound of her low voice got my dick hard, but not hard enough to miss out on money. I simply hit her with a "I'll let you know," before hanging up on her.

She called back a few more times and even sent some texts that all went ignored. Once I was out of work, I went back to the crib and into the backyard where I had a stash spot that held the rest of my shit. One thing about me was you would never catch me with everything I had on me. I was up about three thousand so far, and I never kept all my cash or work on me. Before I ran out, I was always sure to cop up again, so I never faced a drought. The moment I got six thousand dollars, I would give Manny three of it and stash the other three. I knew I would be able to give him the last thousand not long after that. After putting most of my cash up and grabbing some more work, I headed back to the block.

The fiends were coming from every direction, and I was loving every moment of it. Between my phone ringing and walking all around the neighborhood to supply them with the shit they needed, I was on my own high. As I walked back to the block, I watched as a group of guys with black hoodies on walking towards my way. That was never good, and since nobody had been on the block, I knew either they were about to hit the bando or myself. Reaching in my waist band, I cussed myself for not having my gun on me. My dumb ass left it on the bathroom sink when I ran into the house to take a piss. Keeping my calm, I kept walking, because whatever was gone happen was gone happen.

"What's good, boy, what's in them pockets?" one of them asked once they were close enough.

It was only three of them, and if they all didn't have guns trained on me, I would have beat they asses. Looking at each one trying to find something that I would remember about them, I sighed when I couldn't. All their hoodies were scrunched up tight, and all-black gloves and everything wasn't helping.

"Man, I ain't got shit in these pockets for y'all," I let it be known. There was no way they were gone make me out to be no bitch, and I was willing to die over my respect.

"Just give whatever to us so we can leave. We know you was out here all night, so you got to have something. Come up off that shit or we taking it. Either way, we ain't leaving without it," the other one said, and I smirked at him.

My auntie's voice played in my head over and over, telling me to just give them what they wanted, my life was worth so much more. However, my pride wouldn't let me do it. It didn't matter how right she was, my ego was big and if they wanted it, they would have to take it from me. Keeping the same smirk on my face, I prepared myself for a fight.

"Bet, you wanted this," the leader said and struck me with his fist.

The punched didn't do anything but anger me, so my ass swung back and connected with his jaw, stumbling him. I pulled up my pants and swung blindly because it was three of them. I didn't have time to calculate my punches or even make sure them muthafuckas landed. I felt like a cold bitch because I was just throwing punches. And the more I threw, the harder I felt like somebody's hits were. The warm feeling of something leaking down my face and into my eyes was what made it worse. I couldn't see, but that didn't mean I was giving up. After a while, I felt lightheaded and did the best thing, and that was cover my face. One of them pushed me and I could feel myself falling, so I protected my head from the fall and balled up like a damn kid while they stomped me and ran in my pockets.

The entire time, the only thing I could think about was if they didn't kill me, I was going to kill them. Wasn't no way somebody would be able to live and tell the story of how they beat me and robbed me and got away with it, so the next muthafucka could try and pull the same shit. My head was spinning and pounding. I could hear someone screaming my name, but I couldn't respond. I attempted to get up but fell back down, frustrating myself. The moment I got my hands on my gun, a killing spree was going to begin. Every part of the city was gone shed blood until I got them niggas. Attempting to get up one more time, I groaned in pain but stood to my feet. Touching my forehead and bringing my blood-covered hand back to my face, I frowned. Making my way to the bando, I banged on the door until somebody opened it up.

"Yo, what the fuck, dawg, you good?" this dummy had the nerve to ask, like I looked okay.

Pushing past him, I made my way to the bathroom and got a towel and wiped my face. The more I did, the more I became weak. Fighting through it, I wiped all the blood from my face to see a small gash right underneath my hairline. My face was red, and I had sported a nice bump on the side of my head. Yeah, niggas was dying.

"Elise, come stitch this nigga up!" Kilo yelled out to one of the girls he had to bag his shit up that he was also fucking.

Elise made her way into the bathroom and looked in the medicine cabinet to get what she needed. Kilo handed me a Xanax bar, and I quickly took that bitch before the pain really kicked in. Elise made me take a seat on the toilet while she cleaned me up.

"Fuck happened?" Kilo asked, and I ran the story down to him.

"They about to feel me, real shit. When I figure out who they are, the streets gone be hot because I'm shooting first. I don't want to hear shit. All I was trying to do was get my money. I don't fuck with nobody shit, I wasn't even fucking nobody bitch now," I said, feeling the pill starting to kick in.

"I'm 'bouta stitch you up, baby. This alcohol gone burn and ain't shit to numb you with, so you gone have to take the pain. I'm gone have to do at least eight stitches," Elise said before she got started.

Closing my eyes, I tried to prepare myself for the pain. It wasn't as bad as I thought, even though I still felt it. I sat there with my head back the entire time. When she finished, Kilo handed me a bag of ice. Taking it from his hand, I got up and walked home. The entire walk home, I thanked God for sparing my life because they could have killed me. The thousand dollars in work and four hundred dollars they got pissed me off more than the damage that was done to me physically.

Walking into the house, I went straight for a shower and then climbed into bed, placing my gun that I retrieved from the bathroom under my pillow. As tired as I was, I couldn't sleep, trying to rake my brain on anything that could link me back to them niggas. My bedroom door flew open, and I quickly grabbed my gun, cocked it, and pointed it at the door.

"Put that shit down. It's clear you ain't shooting shit," Manny said while flicking on the light.

I put my gun back in its rightful spot and laid back down. Manny took a seat in the chair next to my bed. He stayed silent for a while, and I already knew his ass was waiting for me to fill him in on what happened, so I did while we smoked.

"My thing is, why wouldn't you just give that shit to them? It wasn't worth your life. If that was us on that job, you know what we would have done. Ya pride be getting in the way of a lot of shit. Bro, we just lost somebody, we ain't trying to lose you too. Cuz wouldn't know what to do without you. He already cooped up in that room like he doesn't exist. You got more shit to be worried about. It wasn't even like that was everything you had. You still took the loss and got your ass whooped too. Now peep, get some rest. Tomorrow, bright and early, we on niggas' ass, and don't forget ya gun this time, lil' bro," Manny stated before getting up and leaving back out. Closing my eyes, I let the pill and weed do their job.

❧ 9 ❧

DENVER

I must have rolled over a thousand times. The clock on the wall read 3:06 am and I couldn't sleep. Something was wrong, I just didn't know what. The funny feeling in my stomach kept getting worse as I tried to force myself to sleep for what seemed like the millionth time. Closing my eyes, I tried to relax and work on my breathing, some shit I learned from Justine when I first got here. She said it helped her, but the shit wasn't working for me at all. Hearing the door creak open, I looked over at the silhouette of a person.

"Denver, baby, wake up," one of the staff members said. I couldn't make out which one because the room was dark as hell.

"I'm up, what's wrong that you have to come get me?" I questioned.

"Come with me, I'll tell you on the way." At that point, I had realized it was Ms. Juanita, the lady who worked as a staff member and was nice and cool. She reminded me of the laid-back auntie everybody loved.

Getting out the bed, she pulled me out of the room. I thought we were going into one of the rooms, but she led me outside to her car. I hesitantly climbed in, and she started the car and pulled off. My mind was running a mile a minute, and it was quiet as hell, making me think of the worst. After a while, I noticed we were pulling up to the hospital, which alarmed the hell out of me.

"Yo, Ms. Juanita, what's going on, what we here for? I ain't been sleeping or eating, but I ain't sick, what's going on?" I said to her.

She looked over at me and grabbed my hands. Her eyes were red and glossy. I watched intently as she opened her mouth and closed it.

"Baby, Dakota is here. I'm not sure why or what is going on yet. I know things are looking bad for her and we needed to get you here," she started, but before she could finish, I was jumping out of her car and running inside of the hospital. I didn't stop at registration, I ran right to the emergency department and looked around for anyone that could help me.

"Where's my baby? Where is my baby?" I screamed. The solemn looks on everybody's faces had me feeling a way. Nobody was giving me the answers I wanted, and when the lady who was responsible for my baby walked out in cuffs with her head hung low, I lost my mind. Racing over to her, I knocked her in the face, making her fall sideways. If it weren't for the cop holding her arms, I'm sure the bitch would have fallen like I wanted her to.

"We can't have that. If you don't calm down, we will be hauling your ass off to jail too," he threatened, and I didn't give a single fuck.

"She's a minor and that's her child that's back there, Officer. Please excuse her behavior," I heard Ms. Maria before I saw her.

The officer looked at me with an expression I couldn't read, while Ms. Maria pulled me to the back. I looked in every room I could, hoping one was my baby and she was up and smiling. However, when we got to a room with nurses standing outside the door, a sharp pain shot through my body. The nurses all moved out my way and let me into the room where one nurse was holding my baby. She handed her to me, and I swore she was sleeping so peacefully. I had never seen her sleep like this in my life.

"So, what's wrong? She is just sleeping, right? What was the big deal?" I asked them, looking around.

The nurse looked at me with an expression I couldn't read before walking out of the room. Ms. Maria made me sit down while I kissed on my baby and tried to make her wake up for me. When I felt on her stomach, like I always did when she slept, and didn't feel the rise and fall of her chest, I looked up at Ms. Maria. Standing up, I ran into the hallway with my baby.

"Hey, I need you to help her, please. She's not breathing. Do some CPR, why are you just standing there, please help her!" I screamed at the nurse who was standing outside of the door.

"Denver, she's gone, baby. She has been gone since we got you up. They tried to do all they could to help her."

"How, why? Please, why me? I been through enough. I'm only seventeen and been through so much hell. Why does God keep me here if I'm only here to receive bad? I'm tired of this. Everything has been taken from me. I did what I needed to do to get her back. I hate life, I want to go be with her. She was all I had left. My Kota girl loved me, and I told y'all to check on them. I told y'all on that visit something wasn't right. Y'all claim to help the kids and find them the right places, and look at this. Them people done killed my baby and ain't shit I could do. If y'all would have just left us alone, she would still be here with me!" I screamed while holding my baby to my chest.

Nothing in the world could have prepared me for this. I slid down the wall and sobbed for what felt like the millionth time in my life. The doctor walked into the room and stood there for a second before speaking.

"Hello, I'm Doctor Henry. Your daughter came in today because she was left alone in the bathtub and rolled over into the water for what seems to be a great length of time, based on the water that was in her lungs. She also had some bruises and a trace of a controlled substance in her blood samples. Due to those factors all together, she came in already coding. We did several minutes of CPR on her, which in this case didn't work nor help. The stories from the people whose care she was under didn't make sense, and we had them arrested," he told me with the same blank look on his face.

I nodded my head because it was all too much to take in. I didn't have any questions or anything, because my mind was blank. The only thing I could think of was to kill myself so I could finally be with my baby.

As soon as I thought my life was taking a turn for the better, shit got worse for me. This was the ultimate low for me. Surviving this would take a lot of strength from me, and I was almost positive I didn't have it.

⚜

Two weeks later

"Demi, come on, we would like to see you in the office for a second," Ms. Maria told me.

My heart rate speed up, and my nerves started to go wild. The only time I ever went to the office was when I was in trouble and lately, I hadn't done anything. I had been going to therapy and class, doing whatever else I had to do for them to leave me alone. They had my ass under suicide watch because I kept saying I wanted to die. Since my baby had died, eating and everything else became hard for me to do. All I did was smoke and sleep.

I was praying some more bad shit didn't happen and the thing I feared most didn't occur. Somebody else dying and me having to deal with the pain was something that would quickly make me have a panic attack. Slowly standing up off my bed, I walked behind Ms. Maria. With each step I took, my palms sweated a little more.

"The fuck did I do?" I racked my brain for answers but came up with none, which led me to believe the worst. Treasure's dumb ass done got killed. That thought alone had me about to pass out.

As we got closer to the door, I began to sweat. Walking inside, I stopped at the door.

"Hello, Denver. Take a seat, please," Mr. Howard spoke.

"Mr. Howard, I swear to god I ain't even do shit. I mean, nothing this week. I been on my best behavior, during school and all. Look, you ain't got to send me back with these people," I rambled.

I was finally comfortable with being here, and accepting the death of my daughter was becoming a tad bit easier. I knew everyone and I didn't too much see a need to go to a home when I would be grown soon. The reason I wanted their help was to get my child back, and she was a little too late for that. I could get a job and save my money.

Looking down at my hands, I began to play with my fingers. I knew for sure I wasn't sitting down. I would plead my case until my lips fell off. I knew if they sent me away I wouldn't be here with Justine.

Justine was my best friend, the left to my right, the only person I had left in this world who genuinely cared for me. Justine was there every step of the way after Dakota died. Now my girl needed me, and I would be gone. Being in this place was far from perfect, but it was home for me. I promised myself that if I made it out of here without Justine, I would come back every day, and if it was a home too far away, I would do everything in my power to not go.

After a while, those thoughts were gone because we knew that we were leaving this place together to be able to lean on each other. Now here comes some more bullshit. I wanted a family more than anything but shit, I was almost eighteen, and living here until I reached the age to go out on my own wouldn't be so bad. Hell, I had lost the only blood family I felt any sort of love towards, and it wasn't no gaining that back. My thoughts were interrupted when the lady cleared her throat.

"Oh, my bad. Now, what had happened?" I questioned.

"Denver, that's not what this is about. This is your grand-mother. She will be taking you to your new home. Go ahead and get to know her for a second, then pack your bags." He smiled.

I wanted to slap the smile off his face. I couldn't believe this shit. I was looking for this day to come when I first got here, and now that it was really going to happen, I didn't want it. I sucked in a deep breath and slowly let it out.

"Come again? How you expect me to just leave Justine? She is the only person that has been here for me. I asked y'all to help find them when it mattered the most. My baby is dead now because y'all took her away from me. I needed her then to help me get her back. You're telling me now that the only other person I care for in this world 'bout to be pulled away from me again. Excuse me, grandmom lady, you want to adopt another teenage girl? We will be out your way, I promise," I begged.

The lady shook her head no, and I turned to walk off. Since it really wasn't like I had a choice, I could wait to get to know her. If anything, I had to go tell Justine about this bullshit and have a few last moments with her. I couldn't believe somebody finally wanted me. When I first got here, that's all I dreamed about, but now that I made a sister in here, the last thing I wanted to do was leave her.

"Aye, quick question. How far you live from here?" I asked, turning back to face her.

"About fifteen to twenty minutes," the lady answered with a smile.

I nodded, turning back and running to the room I shared with Justine. I knew she had to be back from the shower at this point.

"Girl, let me tell you what just happened to me. So, I'm sitting here getting dressed, and Ms. Maria takes me to the office. I'm begging and pleading with them not to send me to no other home because I'm cool here. Whole time, it's a lady who supposed to be my grandma that came to adopt me," I got out in one breath.

"A, what? Why? Like, out of all the kids here, why they got to come get you?" She sighed.

"Same thing I was thinking. I ain't even ask, what I do know is they give them some money to keep me. I'm gone see how much I can get from her, and we gone split it down the middle. The lady lives fifteen to twenty minutes from here, so every day we gone meet each other. If they cool enough to take me shopping and stuff, every time I'm gone get you something too. I love you, sis, stay strong. Just because they are separating us don't mean our friendship over," I cried.

Justine looked up at me, and tears fell from her eyes as well. I didn't know what the future held, but what I did know was we were going to be straight. I really didn't want to leave her, but it seemed like I ain't have no choice.

"Denver, let's go," Ms. Maria said.

I hugged Justine one last time before grabbing my bag of very few outfits and heading to the door. I looked back one last time at the place. It was sad to say, but I was going to miss it. Justine followed me to the door where she stood there and watched while I got into the car. The only person I knew that had my back was standing there looking like a lost soul. Sitting my bag in the backseat, I climbed in and slowly closed the door. The entire ride to my new grandmother's house was completely silent.

We pulled up to a small home on a block that was filled with people. She shut the car off and climbed out of the car. Not wanting to be left out there, I got out and followed behind her.

"Look, I know my home isn't the best, but it's clean and you will have your own space. I do have some rules and I would like you to abide by them. We will touch on that in a moment, though. I'm sorry about your child. The moment I found out about you, I did everything in my power to get to you. Time just wasn't on our side. I will be receiving a check for you once a month, which will allow me to take care of you. With that I will give you money, about a hundred dollars a week. What you choose to do with it is on you. I'm your grandmother, Ann, and your father is my son. Had I been known about you I would have come to get you, but I just found out about you. I'm sorry we had to meet like this, but I'm glad we are going to be in each other's life. Your father's name is Maurice. He is currently in jail and should be home within the next year. He was sentenced to ten years in jail, and from my understanding he just learned about you. Whoever your mother is had to have her reasons as to why she didn't tell anyone about you, and if I had to guess why, it would be because of your father's nasty ass wife, Lauren. You have an older brother as well, his name is Emmanuel. He should be by sometime today so he can meet you."

I looked at Ms. Ann and took in everything she said. If that was my mother's reason, then I didn't understand why she did it. No matter who he was married to, I deserved to have my father in my life. It was too late now, and I couldn't ask her why.

"I don't plan on giving you any problems, and whatever rules you have I'll follow. I do want to get a job and if possible, get my license. The less you must do for me, the better. For the record, I'm appreciative of what you are doing for me because you didn't and still don't have to. If you have a curfew set, just let me know and I will be in on time. And I hope you don't mind me going back to see my friend, because that's a must for me. I have to help her because I'm all she has." Ms. Ann nodded her head at my response before taking me upstairs to my room.

I looked around the room and it wasn't big, but it was my own. It held a full-size bed, which was way bigger than the little cot I was used to. There was a small flat screen TV on the dresser and a closet. On the bed was an iPhone and I wasn't sure which one it was, but I was happy to have it.

"It's not much, but it's the best I can do. I hope you like the colors of the room. Your social worker is supposed to be giving me a five-hundred-dollar check sometime this week to take you shopping for clothes and things you need. She said it is like emergency money they give. I'll take you to the mall once I have it and let you get whatever you see fit."

Dropping my bags, I walked over to her and pulled her into a hug. She was a sweetheart and didn't know that she was changing my life by giving me the feel of a family again. I could feel her tears wetting my shoulder as well as me hearing her low sniffles, which made me hug her tighter. She pulled back and held both sides of my face.

"Denver, girl, on my life, I will not let you down. Until the day I leave this world it will be you and me. You are such a beautiful young lady. I'm so sorry things turned out the way they did for you, which is why I'm going to do everything in my power to make shit better." Tears fell from my eyes as I looked at her. She kissed my cheek before walking out of the room.

For some reason, I believed her and was happy that she had entered my life. I laid back on the bed and played around with the phone while thinking of all the clothes I could get Justine and myself. My life was about to be different, I just knew it, and hopefully it wasn't in a bad way. Whichever way, I was looking forward to it.

❧ 10 ❧

ZAMIR

Looking around to make sure nobody else was outside but me and my intended target, I smiled. It had been two weeks since that shit happened to me, and it took all the convincing in the world from Kilo for me to sit back and let people show their hand. When I found out that Blitz, one of the people who frequented the trap, had let his big brothers get the drop on me, I vowed that all four of them had to go and anybody with them would just be a casualty of war.

Pulling the strings to my hoodie tighter with one hand while clutching my gun in the other, I slowly crept around his house to the back door. Twisting the knob, I realized these dumb muthafuckas left it opened. Walking in like I owned the place, I pulled my hoodie off my head. He needed to know it was me coming for his ass, especially since he wouldn't live to tell. The black leather gloves on my hand made it easier for me to come and go without being caught. Taking the steps two at a time, I followed the sounds of loud moans. Gagging at the smell that hit me at the top of the steps, I frowned my face up. When I used my foot to kick the door open, the girl jumped off his lap and covered herself with the sheet that wasn't even on the bed.

Aiming my gun, I shot her in the forehead as she went to

scream. Dumb bitch should have been cleaning her insides instead of letting someone in them.

"Man, what the fuck is you doing?" Blitz yelled like that shit mattered to me.

"Exactly what you and your bitch ass brother should have done to me. You thought it was cool to send niggas at me when y'all living better than me. It's cool, my hustle always gets me to where I need to be, and that's on top. You shouldn't have bothered me," I said before shooting him in the head twice. I shot the bitch an extra time just to make sure she was dead, before leaving out the same way I came in.

One down, three to go was my thought as I ran through the alleyways. It took me two days, but I learned my way back to the trap from his house through the alley. By the time I made it back, Manny's grandma was pulling up to her house. She had a girl with her that I ain't never seen before.

"Hey, Grams, I'll be by to get my plate later," I called out to her before walking the few blocks to my house and heading straight to the backyard. I took the gloves and burned them before burying the gun I had used. I would come back later to get rid of it, but for right now, outside was too hot. Going inside the house, I jumped in the shower and handled my hygiene. I came out the bathroom dressed in some gray Polo sweats and the matching hoodie. I grabbed my Jordan's and slid my feet into them. I put all the weed in a black plastic bag from the corner store, tied it, and tucked it in the pocket in the front of my boxers.

"What's up, Nails," I spoke as we passed each other on the steps.

"Hey, Za. You on your way out?" she asked.

"Yeah," I called out but kept on going.

One day I would pull them two out of that room and take them somewhere, just to get my cousin outside the house besides work.

My stomach was growling but I didn't have time to eat. The

money was calling and I had to do what I had to do. I didn't plan on selling weed for the rest of my life. For now, this was all I had to make ends meet, and they barely met most times.

Making my way out the door, the sun hit me in the face. It was a little windy, which was fine with me. Spring was my favorite time of the year. The weather was perfect, it wasn't too hot nor was it too cold. I walked the few blocks over and went inside of the corner store. I grabbed a bottle of water that would have to hold me over for a little while. Making my way out the store, I went and sat on the steps. The block was now popping because of Blitz's tragedy, and everyone was trying to figure out what happened and who did it. I pretended to want to know as well.

"What's good, Za, you playing the block all day or you going to that party tonight?" Jody, one of the old heads that hung around, asked.

Was he really an old head? No, however, at the age of twenty-seven he hung with all the older people and his name held a lot of weight in Philly, just like Kilo. Yet, he was more into the streets and got his hands dirty. I didn't want to be like him, but I did want to have if not just as much pull as him, then more. He was cool and had all the baldest bitches in the hood fighting over him. I had a few bad ones myself, but they were nothing to brag about. Plus, I wasn't looking to get into anything serious because when I did, I wanted to spoil my bitch and be ready to take her out and whatever else. I couldn't do that right now, though, so I only used bitches to get my dick wet.

"I may slide to that jawn if the block treats me right today. You know I will be out here until the sun come up if I got to be.

What's that I hear about Slim not getting that shipment?" I asked him about his uncle, who supplied Kilo and everyone else. I didn't care what the other people got. Kilo was my concern for the simple fact that I copped from him.

"It's supposed to come through tomorrow. Them niggas over in Cali been moving slow. We trying to find something new, but until then we got to wait," he said as he took a seat next to me and pulled out a Ziploc bag full of weed.

He rolled up while I served a few people. I looked up the street and saw Paulie and her friends walking towards us. Paulie was a little pretty, ratchet bitch that I would have thought about making mine had the whole hood not fucked. She was the type where all you needed was some weed and a few dollars. Her mom was the exact same way, and I was proud to say I hit them both off with the dick. Most times I wished I hadn't, because they both be tripping.

"Za, hey baby," she spoke.

Inhaling the weed that Jody had passed me, I gave her a head nod. She frowned at that before attempting to sit on my lap. I quickly pushed her off me, making her fall down the few steps and land on her ass.

"Fuck is you doing? You know we're not even on that. I keep telling you that shit," I barked.

Paulie looked at me like I had hurt her feelings, while Jody was cracking the fuck up. I sat back down and dusted the ashes that had fallen on my hoodie from standing up. Jody was doubled over laughing while my face had a scowl on it.

"Damn, bro, fuck wrong with you?" Manny asked. I hadn't even noticed him walking up, this dumb ass bitch had me off my square.

"You had to see this shit. He jumped up like ole girl spilled some hot shit on his lap, whole time she just sat on him." Jody doubled over with laughter. The shit wasn't even that funny.

Paulie got up off the ground and placed her hand on her hip while shooting me an evil glare. I would be lying if I said she didn't look good as hell. Her ass looked so much fatter as she rested on one foot, and her weave was fresh, which was probably the reason she brought her hot ass down here.

"You wrong for that. I'm good enough to suck your dick but only good enough to sit on it behind closed doors?" she shot at me like she was saying something nobody knew.

"Pretty much, and so is your mom. Now if you not about to grab no work, you can keep it pushing. It's probably another nigga around that'll wife you up, but it ain't me." I shrugged, being honest.

She stormed off down the street with her group of followers while I continued to smoke and make money. I looked over at Manny, who was unusually quiet, and gave him a questioning look. Instead of him saying anything, he kept quiet and puffed on his weed. Every trap that came, Manny and Jody let me bust until I had no more work left. I was up another four hundred dollars and only two was pocket money. I was using the other part to add to my re-up money. Jody got up and gave us daps before leaving to go grab something to wear to the party tonight.

"So, what's good, bro?" I said soon as Jody pulled off.

"Man, Grams call me this morning on some shit, saying I need to come over to meet somebody." He rubbed his hand over his face, some shit we both did when we were frustrated.

"Okay, and?" I said, not seeing the problem.

"And it's my fucking sister. Apparently, my pops had a child two years after he had me. She was saying ain't nobody know shit about her until DHS contacted her. You know Grams went and bought all this shit and then went and got her. Now she has custody and wants me to meet her. Get this, though, my mom overheard the conversation and damn near lost her mind. The way she was acting was like she probably knew all along it was a possibility I could have a sister. I'm supposed to be there now," he said, looking like he ain't want to go. Knowing Grams, her ass would pull up and cause a scene out here, so he ain't really have a choice.

"Oh shit, look, it can't be that bad. She already here now, so you might as well see her and get to know her. You always wanted a sister, now you got one. I can go with you if you want," I offered.

"That's why you my guy, come on," he said, unlocking his car.

We got up and walked to his Crown Vic. He pulled off and sped the few blocks to his grandma's house. Once he parked, I figure we would get out, but Manny made no attempt to move. After what seemed like forever, he climbed out the car and I followed behind him. We walked inside Grams's door and were greeted with the smell of fried chicken. I made my way right to the kitchen to grab me a plate or two.

"Hey, my baby. Where is my other boy? His behind took all day to get here. I don't know if I want to curse him out or give him a hug. You hungry?" she said, all in one breath.

"Yes ma'am," I replied.

I went upstairs to wash my hands and when I came out, I got a glimpse of who I'm guessing was the sister going into one of the rooms. The only sight I got of her was her plump ass, and my god was it beautiful. I was just hoping her face matched, then again, I was praying it didn't because I couldn't look at her like that. She was my brother's little sister, which would make her family. Running down the steps, I went back to the kitchen and took a seat. Only at Grams's house would you be getting dinner at three in the afternoon. I was thankful for it because I wouldn't have to worry about eating later.

"Za, bro. Come on, let's blow some!" Manny yelled, and I already knew where he was.

Grams had turned the basement into his room a couple years back because she got tired of us smoking on her porch or sneaking in the room and smoking when he stayed over. She figured if she gave him the basement, she couldn't see him, and he had a door where he could come and go without opening her front door, nor would she be able to smell our weed that much. His mom let him do it and Grams felt like she was wasting her breath talking to us about why we shouldn't smoke, and we would just do it anyway right after one of her extra-long talks. Standing up, I made my way down the steps.

"You see your sister yet?" I asked him.

"Nah, I came straight down here. I'm good as hell with females, but I ain't gone lie, sis making me nervous and shit," he told me.

"Man, just go up there and get her. Easy way to get to know her is to see if she smokes."

. . .

Just as I said that, there was a soft knock on the door. Manny got up off the bed he had down there and went up the steps to open it. Making myself comfortable on the couch that was across from his bed, I grabbed the weed and wraps and began to roll up. Looking up to see who was coming down the steps with him, it was his sister.

"So, I can cop from you, or you know who I can get some from? By the way, I'm Demi, and I guess we brother and sister. Nice to meet you, big bro," she went on.

"I know who you are, good to put a face to the name, though. You can either grab from me or Za. Za is my boy, my brother, only grab from him or me."

I nodded my head at her and went back to rolling up. Denver knocked my feet off the couch and took the seat at the other end, making me frown my face up at her. I didn't like people touching me, especially people I didn't know.

"You could have said excuse me," I told her as I sealed the back-woods before lighting it.

"And you could have moved your foot since you see I needed a seat, and you just don't sit on people's bed with outside clothes on," she shot back.

I let out a sigh, trying to control myself. My anger wasn't the best, and I was considered a wild card when I was heated.

· · ·

"Chill, y'all, let's just smoke and talk," Manny said, knowing what was up with me.

I hit the blunt a few more times before passing it. When Denver stood up to pass it to Manny, I couldn't help but to stare at her. She pulled her jeans up that hugged her ass but was loose at the waist. She had on a pair of Ugg boots that you could tell she had for a while because the back of them were going flat, and her white T-shirt fit perfectly, showing off her breasts. I could tell they were about a C-cup, but they were still a mouth full. I let my eyes travel up to her face, and I couldn't deny the fact that she was beautiful. She had a nice pair of plump lips that I wouldn't mind sucking and kissing on. Her slanted eyes and blemish-free skin did something to me. She caught me staring and licked her lips before giving me the finger.

"Hell nah, bro," Manny said as he blew out a cloud of smoke.

I shook my head at him, trying to erase every nasty thought that was going through my mind. She was forbidden fruit, and as much as I wanted a taste, I needed to stay away from her ignorant, bald-head ass.

🜲 11 🜲

JUSTINE

Watching Denver walk out that door had me feeling a pain I hadn't felt in a while. I was alone again, and it was almost my eighteenth birthday. My girl was going with her family and honest to God, I was happy for her. However, that didn't mean that I wished like hell she didn't have to leave. My social worker, Ms. Harrell, said that I had the option of leaving when I wanted to once I hit eighteen, and that I didn't have to leave until I was twenty-one. She didn't even understand that once I hit eighteen, I was gone. It would be time for me to figure life out on my own. I was tired of fearing the what if's and ready to just go wherever life led me. The only person who knew what I had been through was Demi, and that was one of the reasons she promised to stick by my side.

Sitting on my bed, I looked over the photos of my best friend and me. What was only a few hours felt like so much more, and I was missing her. Grabbing my bear pillow and holding it close, I laid down and cried. Today was my last day shedding tears. From here on out, people were going to see the savage in me and not the kindhearted girl that had been showing. The only thing I wanted in life was money and stability. It wasn't the lavishness that I wanted but those were two things I could control and knew wouldn't leave me unless I allowed it, and I craved it.

Getting up, I paced the small room while looking at Denver's bed. I was praying like hell she kept her word, because every bit of money she gave me would be saved up for the day that I decided to leave. It was sad to say, but I wasn't even gone tell her where I was going, I was just going to pack up all my shit and leave. Once I bettered myself, I may come back. Until then, I was going to sit back and plan like a muthafucka.

"Justine, we need you to go into class and not get kicked out this time. I told you before if you needed help with your reading to let me know and I could pull you out and give you some extra help," Ms. Harrell told me as she poked her head into the room.

That was another thing that was gone hold me back from life. I couldn't read to save my life and that was hurting me more than I wanted it to. I wished that I could read when I looked at paper or books, but all I saw was a bunch of letters. My dad couldn't read either, so he was no help with teaching me. I was too afraid to ask for help because people found that shit funny, which was why I would rather figure it out on my own. When Denver came, she would help me and was the only person who knew what was going on with me, and she never told anyone.

Instead of pacing the floor some more, I went ahead and left out the room and down the hall to where the reading class was held. Sitting in my normal seat, I kicked my feet up and looked at the board. Each time I did this shit, I grew more frustrated. I wanted so bad to understand, but I couldn't. I knew basic words and often used the speaker to talk my messages, or I used slang.

"Nice of you to join us today," Chandler's old ignorant ass said with a smirk.

She was one of the adults I came across that I always wanted to knock the fuck out. She was always being smart and knew that I was struggling. Instead of her trying to help me, Chandler would make a mockery out of it and always called on me to read out loud, which would end in me telling her about herself and walking out. Most days I just stayed in my room to save us both the trouble.

"Please keep the smart shit to yourself. I don't want to be here as much as you don't want me to be." Rolling my eyes, I sat quiet for the entire hour I had to be there.

Nobody talked to me or bothered me for the whole time, and I was thankful for it. Once class was over, I headed to the dining hall and ate dinner by myself before returning to my room and climbing on my bed. The time seemed to be going much slower since I had nobody to talk to or no one to be bothered with. I longed for self-love but didn't know how to start or even where to begin to love myself when no one ever loved me in the first place.

"You can't sit in this room every day waiting for the time to pass you by. You are amazing, and even with you being here, you don't let that be a reason to stop you. Denver put up a fight to get you to be able to come with her and even for her to be able to come visit you and bring you gifts. That girl didn't just leave you high and dry, so don't even think like that. I believe if she really had a choice, it would have been to stay here with you. She will be back to see you, I'm sure of it, just keep focused. And if you decide to leave in a few months, which I'm sure you are, prepare yourself. It's a big world out there and just throwing yourself to the wolves with no plan is only going to cause you to self-destruct, baby girl," Ms. Harrell said as she stood in my door looking at me.

I hadn't even realized I was laying there crying until the tears hit my ears.

"You are right, this is a big world, with billions of people, and out of all those billions of people no one seems to give ONE single fuck about me. The ONE person who was supposed to love me unconditionally and give me the world left me because of me looking like his dead wife. It was my fault she died. I know that's what really bothered him and that's what bothers me. It's like, if I would have never come into this world she would still be here, and I wouldn't have to deal with this fucked up way of living. I didn't ask for this. He cared more about losing her. This man never came back to see if I was alive. He could have never even second guessed his decision. I'm positive he would have felt guilt," I got out in between sobs.

Ms. Harrell's small frame glided across the room, and she sat on my bed then pulled me up into her embrace. I was able to inhale her strong perfume while crying my eyes out. Snot fell from my nose, and I instantly tried to pull back, not wanting to mess up her clothes. Ms. Harrell only held me tighter. She rubbed my back while whispering to me that it was okay to cry and that I would be okay.

"How? How am I going to be okay? I have nothing, I have no one. I'm alone and I thought by now I would be used to it, but I'm not. I miss my best friend and I'm sure she is out there happy, living her best life. I want to be happy for her, but I can't help the jealousy that's running through me. I wish it was me. I'm so fucked up that my own best friend's happiness, who's been by my side helping me, is not okay for me because I'm not happy. She was there for me when I wanted to die, she helped me read better, and my selfish ways are allowing me to say fuck her because she finally got an ounce of help, and it didn't include me."

"Baby, you work on that. You can't simply be happy for someone else because you are not happy within yourself. How about this, since Denver is not here to help you with your reading, I will do it. We can make sight words and practice them whenever you want, just to come to my office when you ready and we can sit there for however long you want and go over them and talk. You are not alone in this world, you just feel like it because of what you've been through. You have Denver and me, and when you decide to leave here, I'm sure you will make more friends and family. Family isn't always your blood. You can create a family and you hold on to the ones who are meant to stay and let go off the ones who should not be in your life." Ms. Harrell pulled back and looked me in my face. I could see how genuine she was being, and that made me feel a little better.

"I just want to be happy for the people I should be happy for. Denver deserves this, and I feel like the way I feel could ruin the best friendship that came into my life all because of the inner jealousy. It's eating me up inside," I admitted.

"One day, you will learn to let that go. If you sat down and told her how you felt, she would understand. One thing we all know about Den, is that she is incredibly open and understanding, even though she has a mean side. I'm going to go back to my office now for a meeting. Come see me if you need me." Ms. Harrell stood and walked out.

I felt like a little weight was lifted off me. I laid back and closed my eyes and fell asleep.

12

MANNY

Sitting back on my bed, I blew out a cloud of smoke, as I listened to my dad run his mouth. He was due to be home in the next few weeks and was losing his mind. I had told him about Denver and even sent him a few pictures of her I stole off her Myspace. It was crazy to me how he knew nothing about her.

"Shit's crazy. I been in here for some time, son. I was prepared to come home to a lot of shit, but a fucking teenage daughter wasn't one of those things. I don't know how to even approach the situation, you feel me?" he said, like he really wanted my response.

I hadn't been able to even get much of a word out since he had been on the phone, so I remained quiet.

"Man, if I find that bitch, I'm gone fuck her up. She told me she got an abortion and even gave me the paperwork for her first appointment. I ain't even gone front like I read the papers, though. I saw her name and the address and was like cool. It was too late for me to even stop the hoe. Dumb ass broad disappeared, and I never heard from her again. I'm a fucked-up dad for sure, my nigga. My seed was living foul and here it is we living good. I mean, you ain't have the best life but yo' ass ain't never wanted for shit. 'Cause let's be real, we not filthy rich, I just knew what to do when we came up."

"Pops, wasn't shit you could do. How about the way your ass sitting here explaining to me, you explain to her when you get the chance. She cool as shit too, we be blowing it down together. Man, Za was looking at her and I ain't like that shit. In a way, I feel like ain't too much I can say about it. I know my man, and I can't allow him to do her like I watched him dog a lot of bitches. Lil' sis deserves to be happy now." I finally got a chance to speak.

My dad and I were close as hell. I got away with cursing, smoking, and sneaking girls in the house because I was his son. He made me watch what I did and was extremely strict on me as far as school and the way I handled myself on the streets. Other than that, I was free to do and get what I wanted. When he came home, it was no doubt in my mind he would give Denver the world, especially since he had missed out on most of her life.

"Son, I got to go. They're doing count and I ain't trying to get written up for shit else, especially since the days of coming home are close. I love you, take care of your mom and sister for me," he said, not giving me a chance to respond before he ended the call.

Climbing out of the bed, I headed downstairs where my mom was in the kitchen smoking and talking with one of her friends.

"I'm telling you, I want to meet her because I know it's the bitch Treasure's daughter. She the only one Maurice's ass kept around. I'm just, you know, a little nervous. I don't have no hard feelings towards her, she is a kid and ain't ask for none of this shit. From what his mom told me, she had a baby who was killed by the foster parents, and that's pretty fucked up if you ask me. I just want to help her, you know, give her the knowledge and love a little girl is supposed to receive from a mother. At the end of the day, she is still my husband's daughter, and I will love and protect her as is. I'm honestly scared that she won't be willing to accept me in her life and that's when shit will be messed up, because I would never make my man choose between his child and me," my mom spoke to Aunt Niecy.

"Manny been around her. Have him set some shit up where you can sit down, introduce yourself, and explain to her where you stand. It can't be that hard. But baby, if she anything like the Treasure I remember, she gone be one beautiful, fighting, nasty attitude having ass bitch." Aunt Niecy laughed.

Not wanting to stand there and eavesdrop any longer, I made my presence known. Walking over to them, I hugged my mom first before doing the same with Auntie. Taking a seat at the island and grabbing an apple, I looked over at my mom.

"Look, I can call her and set some shit up for you, but that's all. I won't be there unless she asks me to. I ain't know she lost a child. She doesn't even talk about the shit. I'm gone have to bring that up with her because I want her to feel like she can at least talk to me about whatever she needs to," I said before grabbing my phone and dialing her number. She answered on the second ring. I told her I was on my way to pick her up, and when she agreed, I gave my mom the thumbs up and headed out the door to go get her. Little did they know, I was dropping her off here and going to handle these niggas with Za. His ass was out here going on missions by himself like we weren't a team.

Leaving out the house, I jumped in my all-black Crown Vic and drove the ten minutes to my grandma's house. Za and Denver were sitting on the steps smoking, which made me frown. Her ass was smiling and talking while he looked at her like she was the only girl in the world. I never saw him look at someone like that, and I was glad to know that he had feelings, I just didn't want them to be for my sister. Fucking around with him would bring her more harm than good right now. I knew she might not listen to me, and talking bad about my boy to her wasn't an option. I just wouldn't let them think it was okay to entertain each other in front of me or around me.

"What's up, boy? You good, sis?" I said after rolling my window down.

Za got up first, and then he grabbed Denver's hand and pulled her up off the step, which caused her ass to blush and show off those deep ass dimples. She wiped her ass off and he stared, licking his lips hungrily like she was his next meal. I honked the horn, making Denver put some pep in her step. Zamir gave me his middle finger before calling me a hater.

"Yeah, okay, I'll see yo' ass in a minute to handle that," I called out while Denver got in the car. She was all giggles and smiles.

"Why you ain't tell me about your baby?" I asked her.

"'Cause I don't want to talk about her. It's easier for me to forget that part of my life, and that's what I'm trying to do. Talking about her ain't gone fucking bring her back, and it ain't gone make it easier for me. So, I block it out. I don't want to cry no more, stress no more. Wasn't shit I could do then, ain't shit I can do now," she snapped.

"Look, I'm sorry. I just want you to understand we may just be meeting, but I'm here for you. I ain't gone let shit happen to you and I don't want you to shut down. Blocking it out is only gone cause you more problems in the future, that doesn't help." I tried giving her my advice, but all she did was grab my weed and begin to roll up.

Pulling off, I drove to my house and parked in the driveway. Denver looked at the house before looking back at me with a confused look.

"This my parents' house, my mom wanted to meet you. To get through life, you must let things out, you can't keep them bottled in. I want to see you do well in life, I know you about to get enrolled in school and it is your last year. You don't have even a full year left before you are doing prom and all that good shit. Make the best of it, go to college, make ya child proud of you. Do it for them since they can't do it for themselves," I spoke.

13

DENVER

"Every time I see you, your fucking face balled up. You ain't even that old, so life can't be beating you like that and if it is, do something about it," Zamir said as he stopped in front of me. I was sitting on my grandma's steps doing what I did best, smoking.

It was seven in the morning and his ass was walking around like he would miss something, while most people were sleep. I woke up about three hours ago with my heart racing and my daughter heavy on my mind. The only way I knew how to get rid of those thoughts was to sneak the bottle of Mad Dog out my grandma's cabinet and have a few sips before coming out to smoke.

"And every time I see you, you are minding my damn business," I shot back.

Zamir was fine as hell to me, just staring at him made my panties moist. I wanted him in the worst way, attitude and all. He often was hot and cold with me. The very few times we were around each other he would be laughing and smiling, and then the next minute he would be giving me his ass to kiss.

"One day I'm gone knock that attitude right the fuck up out

you. You don't know who the fuck I am, so watch how you talk to me," he spat, like I gave a fuck about who he was.

"Bitch, you got me fucked up. You ain't nobody to me, all you are is a nigga that's out here every got damn morning and night. You play the block more than you wash your ass. I see how you barely go home, because clearly your ass got some shit there that you don't want to face. So while you're talking about me, you need to handle your shit," I spat.

"Bitch? Who the fuck you talking to like that? You got me fucked up, I ain't none of these niggas you used to. I'm trying to lighten your fucking mood, your ass talking about what I got going on but just came from the shelter. You ain't got shit, just like me," he yelled in my face like I struck a nerve.

"Okay, and what that mean? You're getting tough with a girl. You better go pop that shit with the nigga that put the gash on your forehead."

"I am, they won't be breathing too much longer. So, keep ya eyes open to the news, dumb ass little girl," he said before walking off, and I wanted to punch him in the forehead to open his shit back up. When he walked off, I sat back on the step, needing some more to smoke and drink.

What he said made me wonder if he would really kill them people, and to make matters worse, my ass was even more turned on by the fact that he even said the shit and he looked serious. I looked back at my grandma's house. It was in the middle of the hood, but she kept everything neat, even the grass was cut. Her house was the only house on the block that looked like something. With all the money Manny said they had, I wondered why she lived in the hood while they had a nice house out in Drexel Hill. While we listened to shootings, loud music, and arguing all night, their shit was nice and quiet. Thinking of their house, I thought back to sitting there talking to my stepmom. She was nice and looked young as hell. She smoked weed and let me tell her the parts about my life I felt like sharing. I had to laugh at the faces she made when I

told her about Treasure and the stories she told me growing up.

Walking into the house behind Manny, my nerves grew as I looked around at all the pictures and things on the wall. The house was cleaner than any house I ever saw in my life. It was like you could eat off the floor in here. It was a long way from living in Treasure's house, we had more bedbugs than a little bit. Them shits was practically eating me and my baby alive at one point. On top of that, the mice in there were like family, I could finally see how Cinderella made them her friends in that movie. They were so bold they would run across my bed that was on the floor and wouldn't even run when you stomped your feet. We ain't have no electric—let me stop, we did but it wasn't legal. Then the ceiling in the bathroom had fallen. Like, literally, we had to slide across the wall to make it out the bathroom. I'm talking about if you stood in the kitchen, I could look down at you from the bathroom. So, to see this house with this much space and all of it clean was foreign to me.

"Hey boo, I'm Auntie Niecy and best friends with Patricia. Anything you need or want, I'm here for it. I hope you don't get an attitude like that lady. Treasure's your mom, right? That bitch used to be a piece of work. She used to fight over Maurice like he was hers, whole time, that man was about to be married," she expressed. Honestly, I didn't care what Treasure did over that man, and if they wanted me here to talk about her, then I could kindly leave and walk back to Grams.

"I'm not trying to be smart, but if y'all want to talk about Treasure, y'all can, but I can leave. I didn't come here for that, and what she did to you is not my fault and I have nothing to do with that. I'm just a product of what your husband and my so-called mom had going on," I made noticeably clear.

"You're good, that's not what I wanted you here for. I was quiet for a second just to take all this in. I know you don't have anything to do with it and I don't hold you responsible. This is just a little harder than I think. I don't know what to say to you or how the conversation should start. But an introduction seems to be the best way, so here it is. I'm Patricia, most people call me Trish; you can call me whatever you want. Ma would be nice if you ever get comfortable enough. Your father is my *husband and Emmanuel is my son. I will treat and love you just like I do your brother. Respect is a must, though. If you respect me, I will respect you. We can talk about anything, and if you ever need me just call me and I will come running. I may give my opinion, but I will never steer you wrong, I promise this is a no-judgment zone. I know this is new to you, but we are a tight family, we are there for one another no matter what,"* Trish started, and I listened.

"Okay, well I'm Denver, Treasure is my mom, and I'm guessing Maurice is my dad. I don't know much about him, and I just found out his name not too long ago. I have a best friend back at the place I was just in who I really want to look out for, and I will. My goal is to finish school and get a job. I want to take care of Grandma when she is older because she didn't have to come get me. That's all there is to know about me," I said, not mentioning my baby.

I wasn't comfortable enough yet to talk about her and I didn't want to. Speaking on her could make me cry or bring up bad memories I didn't want to have. Her dying made me even more paranoid with life and always had me feeling like certain situations would end in death. I tried my best to keep the memories of us being happy in my head, but any thought of her would simply put me in the state of holding her for the very last time.

"Okay, well that's a good start. What are some things you like to do? We could do shopping, watch movies, hair salon, nail salon, you name it. We can have a girl's day once a week, just us two, whenever you want. You can also come here whenever you want, and we can turn one of the guest rooms into your room," she said cheerfully.

"I ain't ever been to any of them places to know if I like them. I would like to go get my nails and hair done, mainly my hair because I'm tired of the ponytail and flat irons," I said honestly, and they both sucked in a breath like it was unbelievable.

I looked at them with a slight frown as they grabbed their bags and car keys. Trish motioned for me to follow her, and I did. While we were in the car, Auntie Niecy lit up some weed, so I figured I could roll my own.

"Ms. Trish, you mind if I smoke?" I asked, because I didn't want to be

disrespectful. If she said no, I would just wait till we got to where we were going and then go somewhere to smoke.

"Go ahead and do your thing. Don't tell your grandma, though. She already gives me enough hell with Manny. I don't need no more from her. And I hope you smoking good shit in my car, not that Reggie." She laughed while passing their weed back and forth. I quietly sat in the backseat, smoking mine to the face.

We pulled up to Cherish These Hands, and I smiled. I always used to walk past here or just come in and sit with my mom the few times she could afford to get her hair done here. My mom would tell me one day she would bring me to get my hair done and I believed her, though the time never came. Trish parked her car and got out, so I quickly followed before she could change her mind. We walked in and straight to the back to a guy.

"Hey, bitches, I just saw you two days ago, Tee, and your weave still fresh, so what's up?" he sassed with his hand on his hip and curlers in the other hand.

"Jewel, hey doll. This is my daughter, Denver, and we need to give her whatever she wants done, no questions. I also need her nails and feet done. She's your niece now, so handle her like you handle me, boo." Trish pushed me forward.

"Oh, girlll, Auntie Jewel is about to hook you the heck up. Come on so we can get you washed." He led me to a chair and a girl came up and washed and blow dried my hair. When Auntie Jewel asked me how I wanted my hair, I shrugged and told him just make me look cute and different from the girl I been looking at. He smiled and went to work on me.

It took a few hours but when he finished, the girl that was looking back at me was completely different, and I swore I would stick with this hair color for the rest of my life. The roots of my hair were still black; however, the ends were a spicy red, and the weave that was in my head was to the middle of my back with big beach curls and side bangs. My leave out was pressed to perfection. After thanking Auntie Jewel and promising him to be back, I went and got my nails and feet done. When I walked out that salon, I left the broken girl that went in, or so I thought.

"Dinner is ready, and stay out my damn liquor, little girl," Grandma said, making me jump. For a second, I was wishing I could feel what I felt that day at the salon. It had been two days and the lonely feeling was back. Often, I wanted to go and hang out with Trish just because of the happy vibe I got with her, yet I didn't want to wear out my welcome. Getting up and slowly going into the house, I washed my hands then sat at the table. My grandma usually ate by five because she had to take her medicine. No matter what I was doing, I stopped so we could eat together.

"I'll have some money for you tomorrow. What do you think about therapy?" she asked.

"It's for weak people. They sit in a chair telling people their problems who can't relate and never even been in the situation in hopes to come out feeling better. How can someone who ain't ever lived that life have answers?" I replied.

Grandma ate some of her food before responding to me. She looked at me with a stern look before saying, "Baby, therapy is for the strong. You go when you want to make a change in your life, when you want help. It takes a lot to go there, but they do help."

"Why you ask about that? We talk a whole lot over dinner but never about that."

"Well, because I think you need to go, if I'm honest. You are only damaging yourself by ignoring that baby's death. It happened. You are so busy trying to erase it that you smoke and drink the pain away. You have lost some weight since you been here. Most times you are so quiet and shut down or busy cursing Zamir out when you really like that boy, and I can tell because when he walks his ass up in here or by here, you smile so hard. When you tell someone about yourself you fail to mention you even ever had a child. I know because if you didn't do that, it's no way in hell Manny wouldn't know about Dakota," she said calmly.

Her mentioning Dakota's name made me lose my appetite.

Placing my fork down, I tilted my head to the side and looked at her. Grandma didn't back down. Instead, she held my glare and waited for my response.

"You don't know nothing. I drink and smoke because I want to, not because I need to. There is no need for me to mention MY daughter. I just don't want to keep telling the same story over and over. I fucking failed her, I wasn't there, and you don't know shit about that because you ain't lose a child, none of y'all did. So, if I want to erase that part of my life, let me fucking do it. I dealt with everything alone and I'm doing well. Ain't no therapist gone be able to help me. Every person in my life that was supposed to help me caused me to be here, and I'm sorry for cursing, I'm sorry for drinking up your stuff, but what do you want me to do? Go see another person to cause myself more pain? Can't nobody help me with the thoughts I have of killing myself, and wanting to be with my baby. I don't want to have to think back to the roaches and bed bugs, the constant nights making bottles in the dark, or wondering how to be a mom 'cause my mother wasn't. I try not to think about it because that's when I cry the most and feel like the biggest failure, so I smoke and drink to numb that shit, and I'm not wrong for doing that," I cried.

Instead of my grandmother saying anything, she pushed her chair back and walked over to me and pulled me into a hug. When I looked up, Zamir and Manny were standing there with looks I couldn't read on their faces. Once my grandma let me go, I ran out the dining room and locked myself in my room. I just knew they were all downstairs talking about me.

14

ZAMIR

earing Denver say all that shit made me look at her different. I already knew she was rare, but to me, that made me want her even more. Before knowing that, you couldn't tell me she wasn't a rude ass, stuck-up little girl. I called her a little girl because she acted like one to me. When she ran out, we all stayed in the same spots, just looking around.

"What the hell y'all doing here?" Grams asked.

"We were just stopping by to get a plate before we headed out to handle some stuff," Manny said while I walked out of the kitchen and up the steps to find Denver.

I knocked on her door twice without getting an answer, so I picked her lock and let myself in. Denver was balled up on the bed, crying her eyes out. Pushing the door up but not fully closing it, I took my shoes off and climbed in her bed with her. Usually, she would curse my ass out, but tonight she just curled up under me. I let her cry while I rolled at least three up so when she was done, we could smoke. Maybe fifteen minutes or so went by before her soft sniffles were gone. She sat up and looked at me before letting out a small chuckle.

"I know I probably look crazy right now and look, that's my story, that's me. You think I'm wrong for not wanting to see a therapist. I'm even doing home school, so I don't have to get close to people." Denver climbed over my lap and grabbed one of the duchesses I had rolled.

"Nah, 'cause death ain't easy. My aunt, who was like my mom, just died and I kind of see how blocking it out may help you. I tried that and it just made me angry. I felt like maybe there was something I could have done more of to help," I said while holding on to her since she got comfortable on my lap.

"I swear I hate my life. Like, everything in it seems to fall apart. I just want that one thing I can hold on to and never let go," she whispered.

We sat there quietly just smoking. As much as I wanted to talk to her and open about myself, I couldn't. She needed someone, and even if it was for a moment, I would be what she needed.

"Can we call it truce? This moment right here feels too good to want to argue with you all the time." She kissed my cheek, and I swear I felt like a bitch the way I smiled.

"Yo, get up. All that talking shit cool, but not on his lap. Let's go, Za, them niggas waiting." Manny busted in the room with a mean scowl on his face.

Denver smacked her teeth but climbed off my lap while I stood up and chuckled. I knew Manny ain't mean no harm and was just mad at the fact Denver found comfort in me and not him.

"I'll be back, ma," I told Denver before leaving with a mad Manny on my heels.

"I told your ass not her, not until she grown and can make her own decisions. You seem to be good with every choice I make but this one. Bro, you dog bitches for a living, and my sister not about to be one of them!" Manny yelled as we walked down the steps.

"I'm a grown ass man, you not about to tell me who I can and can't talk to. You act like I was up there trying to fuck her when all I was doing was talking to her—well, letting her talk to me.

Ain't shit going on. That girl ain't fucking with me like that, and if she was, then I don't have to run shit by you. 'Specially not something like where I stick my dick," I shot back, and this man punched me in my shit.

Now, Manny and I fought a whole lot when we were kids, but we had never caught each other off guard like he just did, nor did we hit each other in the face. He was my brother, and I swore I was his. If looks could kill, his ass would be beyond six feet under. Manny stepped back and threw his hands up.

"Don't even worry about that shit, bro, you got it. Let's go bang on these niggas, that's if you still up to it. If not, I can handle that shit by myself. I don't need to watch my back for you, do I?" I asked him, licking the blood from my lip and spitting it on the ground.

"Yeah, okay, you not swinging back makes me feel like I need to watch you," he said, still in his feelings.

Letting him have it, I got in the car and slammed his door. While he cranked the engine, I got my guns ready and sat them on my lap. We drove in silence, and I said a quick prayer for God to forgive me for my sins, because a nigga was about to commit a few. When we pulled up to the corner of the block, Manny hit the lights and rolled the windows down. However, I had different plans and jumped out the car, quietly closing the door. Ignoring Manny asking me what the fuck I was doing in the process. Slowly creeping down the block, I stayed low on the side of the cars. The closer I got, the louder they became. Manny stayed where he was until I was almost at the house, then he began driving. Once he passed me, he let that shit fly out the window. Of course, they shot back at him, missing each shot. While he continued to drive, I didn't expect his ass to bust a U-turn and come back, but he did. At this point, I was standing up and hitting everything I could. Since they were so busy watching the car come back, they never expected me, and I gave all head shots. Manny stopped his car and I jumped in, and he pulled off.

"Why the fuck did you get out the car?" he screamed like I was a child.

"Had to make sure them niggas was dead so they weren't spinning back on us. All head shots are the best." I shrugged.

Manny drove us to a bridge where we wiped the guns off and tossed them in the water. Afterwards, we headed back to his house where we swapped cars.

"Bro, about that shit," he started, but I flagged him and kept it pushing.

I had a long walk home and was trying to hurry up and get there since I ain't have no gun on me. Manny kept trying to talk, but I ignored his ass and started my walk. The entire walk I watched everything around me. Not that I was scared, but because I didn't want to be caught slipping. When I made it to the crib I quickly showered, got dressed, and headed back down the steps.

"If you gone be out there how you are, at least be careful and don't bring none of that stuff my way. You know if some guys came in here guns blazing, I would shit myself," Mikey said, causing me to jump.

His ass was sitting on the couch with the TV on the DVD screen while eating noodles. I knew because I had noodles so much growing up, I could smell them and the flavor they were from anywhere.

"You know I ain't gone let shit happen to you. I would really go on a killing spree. I have your rent money too. I'm proud of you, because I thought I was gone have to come knock yo' ass out and drag you out that room." I handed him a few hundred dollars for rent and for him to take his wifey on a date.

"This is way more than what you are supposed to pay, and please don't hit me. I don't want to have my cousin arrested. You've beat my behind enough in this lifetime that I should know how to fight, it's just you hit too got darn hard." He laughed.

"Man, it's enough. I have a little extra, so you do your thing.

Keep being you, don't let nobody steer you different, take your girl out, and buy you a game or some shit," I told him before rubbing his head like he was a kid and leaving out the door.

I walked back to the block and saw Denver's ass standing there with a plate. Walking up on her, I grabbed the plate out of her hand and stood there for a second. I easily towered over her little ass. Grabbing her by the waist, I pulled her close to me. She went to back up, but I held her tighter. Something about being in her space gave me a warm feeling inside that I didn't want to go away. Looking down in her eyes, I saw everything in a female I feared. The way she was looking back at me told my ass to run far away, because she had me feeling like a whole bitch.

Denver wrapped her arms around my waist and laid her head on my chest. We stood there silently, just wrapped in each other's embrace. Setting my plate on top of the car, I backed us up until my back was against the wall. One of my hands was resting on her big, juicy ass while the other rested on my gun. My trust was all off, yet she had me standing on the block hugged up, something I said I would never do. I had never felt this attracted to a female before, and it was messed up because I couldn't too much act on it. I didn't want to hurt her in ways I knew I could. I also knew my boy wouldn't approve of this. On top of that, I knew what she would be able to do to me. This girl would be able to break my heart or have me out here like a lost puppy. Pushing her away from me, I told her to go home. Denver looked at me with a frown before nodding her head and leaving. I looked after her until I couldn't see her anymore and let out a deep sigh. I needed her ass away from me quick before I took her back to my house and did things to her I wouldn't regret.

✤ 15 ✤

DENVER

"**M**a, what you are cooking all this food for?" I asked my grandmother as she lit the grill in her backyard. It wasn't summer yet, but it was nice as hell outside. Ma Ann had on her floral dress with some flat shoes on and her hair pulled back into a tight ponytail. She was smiling more than I had ever seen her do since I had been here.

"Today's a good day, baby. Have you been looking into the colleges you're going to apply for next year?" she asked me as she took a long pull from her weed, making me look at her like she was crazy.

Now, my grandma preached to us all the time about not smoking or drinking, and how it's not good for us. But whenever she came out in this backyard and swore she was alone, her ass would be sitting in her chair smoking up a storm. Instead of saying something, I would act like I didn't see her. Here she was doing it without a care in the world. I went over to my grandma and kissed her forehead. In such a short time, I had grown a lot of respect and love for her.

"Your brother supposed to be coming over to take you shopping. Za may be with him. I see how yo' hot ass be staring at him too. That boy is fine as hell, I will not lie, but my Za is a hoe. He be having so many damn girls I done gave up on him finding love. Your brother too. He be thinking I don't know about them having all of them little hoes up in my basement because he got his own entrance," she told me as I sat on the chair next to her.

"Don't nobody be looking at Zamir like that. He's okay look-ing, and he's fun to be around. He listens to me, but that's all it is," I lied. That boy was gorgeous, and the thought of him having hoes just didn't sit right with me. I wanted him for myself.

"Who the hell you think you fooling? Anyway, I told your brother to take you shopping. I already placed your half of the money in your bank account. I love how you want to go and help your friend, but don't give her everything you have. Save some for you just in case you ever need it." My grandma put her weed out and stood up to flip the short ribs she had on the grill.

"Okay, I hear you," I told her, and she rolled her eyes.

"Yo, Granny, you are throwing down," I heard Za say from behind me.

A small smile spread across my face and before I could wipe it off, Grandma Ann was sending me a knowing look followed by a smirk. Zamir walked over and pulled her into a hug and kissed her cheek. I wished like hell it was me that he was holding on to and not my grandma. Nobody would ever know that shit though, with his fine ass. I tried not to look over at him, so I kept my eyes focused on the food that was coming off the grill. Manny's ass was never on time, and if I'm right around the corner but still in bed was a person, it would be him. Zamir walked past and his scent hit my nostrils, making my mouth water. Everything about him just did something to me. Today he wore a pair of seven jeans and a Polo T-shirt, and on his feet were a pair of white Air Force Ones. He looked good enough to eat, and a slight frown grew on my face when he picked up his ringing phone and got to smiling.

"Chill, I'ma get with you later. I promise, just relax. I got some stuff to handle but I'll definitely pay you a visit when I'm done, so answer your phone," he spoke before hanging up. He went to pull me into a hug, but I dodged it.

Standing up, I all but stomped my ass back in the house. I stopped in the kitchen and got a cup of blue raspberry Kool-Aid. Leaning against the counter, I watched as Zamir made his way over to the back door and inside the house. He stopped a few feet away from me and just looked at me.

"Fuck you always do that for? Yo' lil' ugly ass get to stomping ya feet and slamming doors every time you see me caking on the phone." He frowned.

Rolling my eyes towards the ceiling, I let out a low chuckle. I wasn't sure who he thought I was, but his ass was about to find out if he kept playing with me.

"Let's not get crazy. You, for one, know for sure I ain't ugly, that's why you always staring at me, and two, I don't give a fuck about them little dirty bitches you be fucking. You know like I know, if I wanted, I would have your ass on lock. Don't play with me. I'll go fuck one of your friends at the trap and let them tell you what you missing out on." I smirked when I saw his jaw clench and his face turn red.

Zamir walked over to me and got in my face. Our lips were damn near touching, causing me to suck in a breath. If he kissed me right now, I would be willing to give up the goods right on my grandma's counter while she was out back.

"Play with me if you want to and watch I knock that nigga the fuck out. You wouldn't be able to do shit with me, with your young ass, and I can tell just by how I got your ass breathing and I ain't even done shit to you." He laughed and backed up.

I watched him as he made his way into the basement, probably to smoke. He was saying all of that, but I could feel his manhood growing on my leg while he was all in my face. Turning around, I walked upstairs and climbed in my bed while playing on my phone. I was bored out of my mind and was tired of waiting on Emmanuel's ass. Soon as my eyes started to close,

Manny came and plopped his ass on my bed. He kicked his feet up like he didn't have on any shoes, so I knocked them down.

"Quit fucking playing." I frowned when he put his legs back up and crossed them.

"You ready to go? I want you to go to the mall. I'm gone give you five thousand dollars for this month. You can spend, save, whatever. I'm gone be watching what you do, though. I'm not rich right now, but I'm well off and want to make sure you good too. I expect you to blow a bag with this one, but each time I or someone else gives you money, you need to make sure you save some of it. Don't ever let your account reach zero," he told me as he tapped on something on his phone. A couple seconds later, my phone dinged, indicating that a transfer had been made to my account.

Opening it, I quickly put two thousand from Manny and half of the money my grandma gave me into my savings. Standing up, I walked over and pulled Manny into a tight hug. Tears burned the brim of my eyes, but I quickly wiped them away. No one had ever given me that amount of money before and honestly, I didn't know what to do with it. I knew for a fact I was putting some up because I didn't want to ever be flat out broke again. And I damn sure wasn't ever trying to have another hungry night. We got up and made our way downstairs and out the door. Just as I climbed in the front seat of Manny's car, Zamir came and climbed in the backseat. Usually, he would mess with me, yet the entire ride he only talked to Manny. His petty ass even made sure to roll every Dutch so that he wouldn't have to pass it to me. My eyes grew big at the sight of the mall. I had been to a few plazas to shop, but this was my first time coming to an actual mall.

"This might sound dumb, but what stores are in here? Do they have Victoria's Secret in here? I never been to a mall before," I whispered to my brother, who was looking at me like I was crazy. That wasn't something I was proud of, but it was the truth, and I wasn't a person who acted as if I was something that I wasn't.

"Nah, fuck that baby girl, we 'bouta blow a bag. Ain't an area in this mall we not about to touch. If you see a store you want to go in, just go in that bitch, I'm 'bout bless you. If there is something you want, get it, no matter the price," Manny told me with a serious face. I never knew exactly how much money this family had, but I knew it was a lot. Or enough to be buying whatever we wanted without worrying about when we would eat or if the lights would be cut off.

"You sure? I don't really need that much, a few outfits is cool. What you gave me is enough to hold me over for the next couple months. I'm okay with what I have, and I appreciate you for it more than you will ever know. When I get right, I promise to give you triple this." My eyes filled with tears.

"I just need you to stay focused and graduate school. Make it to college and do your thing, get a degree, and become the best version of you, you can be. You will be the first one in the family to go all the way. We are counting on you to carry the family the right way." Manny pulled me into the mall and we went crazy. I had so many bags that I had to keep going back to the car. Zamir's mad ass even ended up carrying some of my bags for me.

Once we finished, I asked Manny if he could take me back to my old foster home, and instead of him agreeing to do it, he drove home, got his other car, and let Zamir drive me. The entire ride, he was quiet and often looked over at me. He would open his mouth like he wanted to say something, but instead of him saying it, he wouldn't say anything at all.

"Right here, I'll be back out in like twenty minutes, if that's okay," I finally spoke.

"Okay, take your time." He leaned his seat back and pulled out his weed, and I knew his ass was gone sit there and smoke until I came back.

Climbing out of the car, I grabbed the bags of clothes and shoes that I had gotten Justine and headed inside the building.

"Hey, Ms. Shavonne, I came to see Justine. Is she in her room, or is she allowed to come out? I brought her some stuff," I said, showing the bags.

Ms. Shavonne smiled at me before standing up and pulling me into a tight hug. She spun me around as if she hadn't seen me in years. I smiled back at her and sat my bags down as Ms. Maria walked in.

"Oh, my good lord, my evil baby is in here with a smile on her face. How you been doing, girly? I'm so happy to see you back. I know Justine is going to be super happy, come on back." Ms. Maria helped me with the bags and walked me to Justine's room. Justine was laid across her bed looking through a book, and I was proud of her at that moment. Getting her to look at a book was hard as hell.

"Best friennnndddd," I called out, and her head snapped up. Justine jumped off the bed and we ran into each other's arms. We hugged so tight and cried for a second before letting go.

"I brought you some things. How have you been? I miss you so much. I couldn't wait for this day. I hope you like everything," I rambled while handing her all the bags. Justine sat on the bed and went through them, smiling at all the stuff I had gotten her.

"Girl, I ain't ever had no damn Victoria's Secret panties. These probably about to have me feeling good, 'cause these Walmart panties be having my thighs on fire." She wiped at her tears.

I had gotten her a few pairs of sandals, some Jordan's, and Nikes. Plus, some clothes and underwear. Justine finished looking at the stuff before she hugged me and thanked me again.

"You really don't understand how much this means to me. I have missed you too, how is your family? I have been having my days in here, but it will get better. I'm gone be old enough to leave here soon, and I'm thinking about having a job before I'm old enough to leave, just to save up as much as I can so I can rent a room or an apartment. That's why I'm focusing on learning to read. I need that to be able to get a job. You meet anybody cute out there? You met any new family, what's up with you?" Justine asked.

"Girl, so my brother has this friend, his name is Zamir, and when I tell you this man is fine as hell, like he is beautiful. Everything about him is amazing, besides his nasty ass attitude. He is like super mean and quiet, though. I know he like my ass too, I can tell by how he be staring at me. My brother cool, I met him. I've met his and talked to her a few times on the phone, she's cool. My grandma is the best, though. Like, I've really grown to love that lady. I'm proud of you, keep striving. Zamir's mean ass waiting outside for me. I'm gone try and come back in like a week or so to drop some more shit off." I reached in my bag and handed her five hundred-dollar bills that I had been holding to give her.

"I always told you I got you when I got it, sis. Please take care of yourself. I'll be back, I love you." I kissed her forehead and she walked me to the door.

Once I was back in the car, Zamir handed me the weed and I took a pull. We sat there for a second before he pulled off.

"What you just did was cool, made me look at you different. Your mean ass is nice in a way to somebody, because you hot and cold with me. Whoever your friend is should appreciate you so much. Ain't too many friends like you and your brother in this world." He smiled at me, showing off them beautiful deep dimples. I just knew if we created a baby, he would have them same ones.

"Thanks, I try. If roles were switched, I would like to believe she would look out for me too," I told him.

Zamir came to a red light and stopped. He turned and looked at me before biting down on his bottom lip as his eyes traveled my body. Leaning over, he kissed my lips, and I almost melted into the seats. He tried to slide his tongue in my mouth, but I backed up since I had never kissed a boy like that. With my baby dad, we got straight to business. There was never no kissing involved.

"I don't know how to kiss like that," I admitted.

Zamir looked back at the road and then pulled over, putting the car in park. He pulled me over to him, and I was now sitting in his lap. He held both sides of my face before crashing his lips into mine. This time, instead of just trying to shove his tongue into my mouth, he licked my bottom lip, and I opened my mouth. I slowly followed his lead and before you knew it, I had caught on. Zamir pulled away first this time and just stared at me.

"Girl, I'm gone need you to get up. As much as I would tear your ass up, I can't do that to you, not right now," he said like he had a change of heart.

Climbing off his lap, I sucked my teeth and plopped down in the seat. Zamir looked at me and shook his head before pulling off.

"I'ont know why the fuck you shaking your head for, like you be on all weird shit," I yelled at him.

"You right." He chuckled, doing double the speed limit all the way to my grandma's house. My ass was scared as hell the whole time too, so I remained quiet. Every time his ass turned a corner, I felt like the car would flip. I thanked God and jumped out the car soon as he parked it. Storming into the house, I was surprised to see it full of people I'd never seen before. It looked as if my granny was throwing a party and it was in full swing.

Zamir shook hands and spoke to people while I searched for my grandmother or brother. I found them in the back yard laughing and smiling. When I walked over, they all grew quiet, making me feel weird. I looked at Ma Trish and she came over and pulled me into a hug. My eyes were locked on the man behind her, and his were on me. I could see him trying to blink the tears away, but they fell instead.

"Wow, nobody couldn't tell me this. Nobody couldn't prepare me or ask me if I was willing to be a part of this? Y'all don't think this could have been done at a different time?" I questioned before storming off, finally letting tears of my own fall. I knew that was my father without anyone telling me. What I didn't know was why today of all days, with all these unknown ass people, did they want him to meet me. I felt like all this was a bunch of bullshit and should have been ran by me first. It was like everybody was saying they wanted me happy but was making decisions for me instead of including me.

❧ 16 ❧

ZAMIR

Denver had been growing on me, so spending time with her became almost a priority. Every day we would eat breakfast and chill together on the block. We didn't know each other for that long, but the shit didn't matter. I knew she was down for me, and I didn't want to fuck that up. I tried my best not to answer calls around her because I knew she would get mad. Like now, we were sitting on the block while she held my gun and watched my back. Manny wasn't too fond of her being out here, but she wouldn't listen to him, and no matter how many times I made her go home, she would bring her ass back. Today we were just chilling and were supposed to go to the movies to see this dumb ass movie she wanted to watch. First, I had to give Manny his money back, so she had to wait until tonight so that I could make the right amount of money to do what she wanted. I had enough money stashed away, but I wasn't touching that for nothing or no one.

While Denver rubbed her fingers over my waves, she talked about how her friend Justine had up and left the place without saying anything to her, and how it hurt her feelings, for the third time since we had left the place this morning. My mind drifted to the offer Kilo gave me. His ass was loving how Manny and I killed those men, and no one was coming after us. I had made sure to take out everyone I thought was connected to them that would move for them. I wasn't a killer at heart but if the price were right, I couldn't say I wouldn't take him up on his offer.

"Za, here come your little girlfriend." Denver pointed towards Paulie, who was coming up the street with her little friends like always.

Every time I encountered her, I wished I could un-fuck the bitch. Paulie just didn't know when to stop. I hadn't seen too much of her since our last altercation and from what I heard, she was messing with some nigga on the other side of town, and I was happy as hell for them, no lie.

"Where the fuck you been, and is this bitch the reason you ain't fucking with me no more?" she hollered like we weren't a few feet away.

This was one of the things I hated about Paulie. She had to cause a scene every fucking time she saw me like we made claims on each other. Looking her over, I frowned my face up and turned back to Denver to finish our conversation.

"Zamir, don't make me smack this bitch just to show you what the fuck I'm about, because you clearly forgot." Paulie stepped closer and so did her friends.

"Za, you better get her. She got one more time to call me a bitch and I'm gone show her what's up with me. I'm not even fucking with you, and you got these overly hype bitches coming at me. Now Miss, your problem is clearly with ZAMIR, so keep it with Zamir," Denver finally spoke, and her voice was soft and sexy as hell.

I didn't know if Denver could fight, but she talked a good game. I knew for a fact Paulie's hands were nice and if she began to lose a fight, her followers would jump in. That was all cool, but if they even thought it was gone slide with Denver, I was gone show them better than I could tell them.

"Okay, miss pretty girl. You may be pretty, but ya face about to be pretty fucked up," Paulie kept going.

Denver sat her phone down and when she stood up, so did I. Before Paulie could utter another word, Denver swung and hit her in the mouth. They way Denver was on her was making me proud; however, Paulie was getting her shit off too.

Denver put her leg behind Paulie's and pushed her back, causing her to fall, and the followers took that as a chance to jump in. Without thinking twice, I began to toss them bitches damn near across the street.

"I swear to god, one of y'all bitches touch her and I'm gone beat y'all ass. Now try me, I swear I don't hit bitches but for her, I'm willing to lay y'all asses out," I barked at them.

Vanessa's dumb ass took me for a joke and snatched Denver by her hair, making her fall backwards, and before I could even think of what I did, I knocked her dumb ass out.

"Bruh, what the fuck," Jody yelled as he ran up and grabbed me.

"Get the fuck off me. These broads got me fucked up thinking they about to come down here with the dumb shit. Then they trying to jump my bitch like I won't kill over her," I expressed.

Jody let me go and stepped back with his hands up. He went to go break the fight up, and I walked up on him.

"I'm just trying to stop this shit, the cops coming." He pointed to the patrol car up the block.

I grabbed Denver. While picking her up off the floor, I slid my gun off her hip and tucked it in one of the car tires.

"Walk off." I kissed her cheek and let her go.

The cops pulled up and assisted the girl up off the ground. She instantly told them that I was the one to knock her ass out, and they came over to question me. Denver came back instead of leaving like I told her to, which made me kiss my teeth.

"Ain't you Rodney's baby mom?" The officer looked at Denver, who was now staring back at him like she knew him from somewhere. The way they were looking at each other piqued my interest.

"Nah, Rodney ain't my baby dad," she quickly denied, and even I knew she was lying.

"Yeah, you are, my dad and mom doing time behind you. They got your fucked up ass baby, and she died and y'all blamed them," he fussed.

Denver's mouth dropped. She opened and closed it like she wanted to say something, but nothing came out. This guy kept talking, so I figured I would help her out. With all my strength, I cocked my fist back and punched him, landing right on his chin. I swear they should have called my ass Knock Out the way I be putting muthafuckas to sleep. Denver stepped in front of me when the other cops came rushing towards me with their guns drawn. Grabbing her by the waist, I moved her behind me.

"Look, whatever happens, happens. I have ya brother money in my book bag inside the back room, it's also money in my room in the closet. I want you to take it and hold it for me. Give ya brother his shit. Make sure you don't let nobody have you like I should. I think I love you. Make it for me and Dakota," I said, giving her one last look before they knocked my ass to the ground.

I covered my head as they kicked and punched me, all the while they screamed for me to stop resisting. Denver was yelling for them to stop. I just prayed her ass stayed back since I couldn't see her. I hated the look on her face after I got my ass beat, they cuffed me, and tossed me in the back of the cop car. I already knew it would be a while before my ass saw the light of day, and I was okay with that. I just wished I could have killed that nigga for what his parents did. Babies were innocent and shouldn't have to go through abuse.

"What the fuck is going on?" Manny yelled, and by the way he came up, I knew someone had called him.

I watched as he tried to come over to the car but was pushed back. Denver ran to him and must have told him what happened, because his ass started to flip out. The car I was in gently pulled off, and I watched them in the distance. I didn't know how I felt about Denver, but I knew I wanted to protect her, and see what it was like to be the person she longed for and needed. The only thing that bothered me was that I was giving the next nigga a chance with her. I knew big bro was going to be fucked up behind this too. It was a choice I didn't regret making and would do it again, so he really didn't have no choice but to understand. I would do the same for him. Closing my eyes, I sat back and enjoyed what I knew would be my last car ride for a while.

❧ 17 ❧

DENVER

Zamir going away broke my heart. Just when we were getting close, he was taken away. I knew he was coming back one day, and I would make sure he was straight. Since I didn't have a job and all I did was hang with him and do home school, going to get his money and moving his work for him didn't sound so bad. I knew everything from watching him do it, so it should be easy. Manny would be upset with me doing it, but if he got on the block with me then he wouldn't have to worry about my safety. Since Za had looked out for me, it was nothing for me to feel like I owed him to do his dirty work until he was released. Whenever he came home, I would hand him everything over. Of course, I would see some money out of it, but majority would be his.

"Get in the car," Manny sternly told me.

Ignoring his command, I watched the cop cars pull off before walking over to the car and getting Za's gun and tucking it back into my waist band. When I was sure it was covered, I jumped in the car and waited for Manny to get in. Once he did, he pulled off and headed the opposite direction of my home.

"Yo, pull the fuck over. I ain't going by your daddy house. I'll see Trish whenever she free from him," I spat when I saw where he was going.

Manny ignored me and kept on driving, so to get his attention, I pretended to open the door and he slammed on the brakes, causing my body to jerk.

"You on some dumb shit. Now I sat back and let y'all do y'all, but you out here acting dumb. My man just went to jail behind you."

"And you act like I told him to. Since he did, though, I'm gone make sure he straight. Which is why I need you to hit the block with me. Let's get this money how he would. We can make a deal too, 'cause we both know he gone do some time for hitting Rodney's dumb ass cousin. That man still getting to me even in his death. But check this, I can bag the product and sell whatever. The cops won't ever suspect me because I'm a girl, long as I stay low key and finish school. Home school boring, so it ain't like I can make friends. Ain't shit for me to do but be up under you now, since you don't got a girl and all the bitches that hang around mad 'cause I had Za." I laughed, yet he didn't find shit funny.

"Man, your head gone. You barely know him and you ready to do all this. That's my boy, he a good dude, so I'm gone make sure he straight. What I can't seem to figure out is how the hell y'all build a bond this strong this fast." Manny looked over at me for a second.

"I don't know. He just was easy to talk to, fun to hang around. He listened to me, he didn't talk or anything he would just let me vent. Plus, that boy is fine as all hell, like God had a special recipe when he put him together." I smiled.

"Look, if I do this with you, you got to do me one favor," Manny said as we pulled up to his house.

Without him even saying it, I knew exactly what he wanted. Sucking up my feelings, I got out the car. I owed this to myself, and this man owed it to me. Taking my time walking into the house, I went in the room that slowly became my favorite. Yeah,

I bypassed everyone inside the home without speaking. Oh well, I didn't have time for manners, and I really didn't care to use them.

"Aye, if you want to talk, let's talk. I ain't got all day," I told Maurice, who walked by the room.

This man doubled back and looked at me like I grew two heads. He let out a deep chuckle and stepped inside the room. We had a silent stare off, and let's just say he looked away first. He was hell bent on having a conversation with me and everyone around this bitch was pushing for it. Now that he had a moment to have it, he was standing there staring at me like I would disappear.

"Look, either we gone stand here and talk or I can be on my way, either is fine with me," I sassed.

He let out another chuckle, which further annoyed me. I went to open my mouth and speak, but he raised his hand, silencing me.

"What you gone do is sit your ass down and listen to me." His voice wasn't angry but very commanding, so I sat my ass down and listened.

"First of all, we gone have an understanding. All that shit flying out your mouth either gone stop or I'm gone pop you in it like the child you are. I'm not here to be trying to control you or no other shit, but you will fucking respect me. We can be cool, or we can go at it every time we cross paths. Either one is fine with me." He used my words back on me.

"Now, I'm gone tell you this. Had I known about your ass, I would have been in your life. Your mom told me she got an abortion, even brought me the paperwork. I ain't bother to see if she had the procedure done. I saw her name, the date, and the address to the place she went to and believed her. After that, she got ghost. It was like her ass disappeared, and I ain't try and search for her because my wife wasn't and still isn't worth losing. I'm here now, if you will let me be. We can work on building something, and it don't have to be rushed either. I want to be the parent you never had. You remind me of myself with your attitude and mouth," he told me.

"It's messed up. Like, I come here and see how my brother been living and to hear you explain why you wasn't there just making my hate for that lady grow. She could have just told you, or did you tell her to get an abortion?" I questioned.

"I ain't tell her shit. We never really talked about anything. At the time, Trish's ass was sneaking around to see me because her parents ain't fuck with me, and they still don't. Treasure was the opposite. She basically was doing whatever with whoever." He plopped down on the couch that was in the room.

"All y'all smoke weed," he yelled when he saw me grab the lighter off the nightstand that I had been looking for.

"After all I been through, weed is only a small problem of mine. Life been kicking my ass, and I feel like I'm in a place to win, thanks to this little thug I met, but now he ain't here and I feel like he ain't here for a reason. Manny don't see it that way, but Zamir was helping me, you know. He taught me how to hold a gun, bag up, pick locks, even helped me with my damn math homework. What got me the most because he never even tried stuff with me, we just naturally kicked it. Now he's gone and as much as it's bothering me, I can't show it," I explained.

"Look, how you feel is how you feel, and if it feels right, then go with that. I'm not here to judge you. You make decisions and I will be there when it's time for you to learn from them, if that's what happens. It seems like he was teaching yo' ass how to be a female thug." He laughed.

"He was, but he was also making sure I got my work done for school too. I probably wouldn't have been graduating if it wasn't for him. I don't even care to go to graduation. Grandma mad about that, but ain't no reason to go, ain't like I got friends."

"Did you try making some?"

"Nope, Za was my friend and all the girls around here want him or my brother, so I ain't the friend for them. I kind of like you, old man. We gone be cool, but I got some work to tend to and it can't get done without me." I stood up and this man pulled me in for a long ass hug. Like one of those hugs where you see somebody you ain't seen in a long time. The moment he let me go, he stared at me for a few more seconds then walked out.

As soon as he was gone, I found Manny and we headed to the trap after he took me to Za's house to get everything I needed. Once we were back in the car, I tossed the stack of money in his lap.

"Za was gone give that to you." I closed Zamir's backpack, leaving the rest of the money inside of it. I wasn't sure how much it was, but I would hide it and return it to him when he was out.

Inside the trap we got to work. I bagged and counted everything out. I was on a mission, to use the little Za taught me and make something big of it. I knew his goal was to out hustle every hustler to be at the top, and I was gone do what I could to make it a little easier for him. When he came home, I would rightfully hand my spot next to Manny to him with ease.

"Sis, you bag up fast as hell. If you learned how to cook this shit, it's over," he spoke.

"Ain't no harm in trying, right? Look, here's what we gone do. Kilo give it to us, right, you can go to Pops and get the direct connect. I can pay that crackhead, Carrie, to show me how to whip that shit up, and we take off from there."

Manny nodded, agreeing with me. What we didn't know was what was in store for us. Yet, I didn't care. I felt like I owed this man because he did something for me. Only time would tell if we were able to handle the fast life, and I was more than ready.

❧ 18 ❧

JUSTINE
TWO YEARS LATER

For the last two years, I dealt with all kinds of rejection from jobs to public housing, anything you could name of. Turning eighteen wasn't all what I thought it would be. Life wasn't getting easier for me. This wasn't what I imagined, and getting by with my little job at this motel was taking a toll on me. I did more cleaning than a little bit and my pay wasn't that great. It was enough to keep me inside a small studio-sized apartment and enough to eat twice a day. Every day I wanted to say fuck it all and just give up. Yet, each passing day, I looked myself in the mirror and saw a reason why I shouldn't. I often thought about Denver and where she was at in life. If she was still upset with me, because if I knew her like I thought I did, she was pissed when she figured out I was gone. Not much time went by, but it felt like years since I had seen her.

"Excuse me, sweetie, I just wanted to know if you liked women. My husband and I are visiting here for a few days, and you fine as hell. Wait, how old are you?" a lady walked up to me and spoke.

I was seated on a bar stool, sipping my drink and minding my business. My neighbor, Blu, had just went to the bathroom and probably got caught up with a female. He often told me how I would make a killing down here if I stopped being shy and got me a sugar daddy. Especially after I let him sample the pussy a few times. Hell, my ass got lonely, and he was borderline cute. When the drinks kicked in, he looked even better.

This lady had caught me by surprise. Never in my life had a female stepped to me, so me being with one hadn't happened. She looked good as hell, and the way she was licking her lips made me want to put this kitty in her face.

"Thank you, I'm Lisa, twenty-one, and you are fine too," I replied, ignoring everything else she said. Giving her my real name and age wasn't an option. Hell, I was in here with a fake ID.

"Look, we willing to pay you a thousand dollars if you okay with coming back to our room. I just need to see proof you clean." She shrugged like it was nothing.

I looked at her with a sour face as her husband walked over. He looked at her with so much love before pecking her on the lips then speaking.

"Trish, what your ass doing?" He licked his plump, juicy lips.

"I'm making us a new friend, if she can show me her records." She smirked at him, and he let out a low chuckle.

Pulling out my phone, I opened my app for my clinic and showed her all my negative results. Hell, a thousand dollars would come in handy.

"Good, and if you taste as good as you look, we can do this every week." She grabbed my hand, and I quickly threw my double shot of Cîroc back.

All three of us walked out the club and climbed inside of an all-black Range Rover. I had sunk into the leather seats, enjoying the feel of them. They talked and giggled while I remained quiet, thinking about if I was about to do this. The money was quick and easy and could get me to where I wanted to be in no time. Since I had no calling, I tried some of everything, and nothing stuck. Hair and makeup were not my thing, and neither was dancing, so stripping was out the window.

"Take this and loosen up, it's an E pill. I only take them when I want to be up for a while and have a good night. It's a mood enhancer, but don't get addicted to them." She handed me a pill with a Superman logo on it. Now I knew I shouldn't just be taking shit, and it might sound dumb, but what could it hurt? At this point in my life, I felt like whatever was gone happen to me was gone happen. Popping the pill in my mouth, I sat back and enjoyed the rest of the ride.

When we made it to the room, I felt a burst of energy. We took a few shots and got right to business. I had finally gotten a good look at this man, and his ass was fine as all hell. The way he looked at his wife gave me butterflies. Hell, I wished someone would look at me like that. I stood off to the side as they shared a sloppy kiss. Since I wasn't experienced with no shit like this, I ain't know what to do.

Trish's pretty ass grabbed me by the waist and kissed me dizzy. When she eased up my dress and slipped off my panties, she released the beast in me. I didn't know if it was the pill or drinks, but the three of us went at it all night, and I loved it. That old man was packing something lethal. He fucked me so good, yet I wanted him to sex me like he sexed his wife. When we were done, he was knocked out cold. She slipped me her number and my money and sent me on my way. I called myself an Uber and went home. My ass couldn't sleep. I washed my body twice and even smoked, and still was wide awake. Saying fuck it, I went over to Blu's house and used my key to let myself in. His uniform was hanging up, letting me know he had worked today. Blu's ass worked as a cop and never wanted anybody to know since he pimped bitches out for extra money. That's why his ass worked in Philly but lived in Atlantic City.

I climbed in his bed and moved his folders. He had a major case he was working on, and I didn't want to mess that up. Climbing onto his lap, I kissed on his neck. I was so horny, and Blu could fuck me to sleep. I rocked my body back and forth on his lap until he woke up and hungrily kissed me. Blu flipped us over then licked and sucked on my neck. He pulled my pajama pants and panties off, and since he was already naked, he slid inside of me.

"Fuck, this shit tight, but I know my pussy. You fucked somebody else?" he stopped his movements and asked with murder in his eyes. My ass got scared for a second, so I did what was best.

Pulling out three hundred dollars from my bra, I handed it to him. He let my legs drop and looked at the money, a smirk formed on his face, and he pulled out of me.

"You don't know what yo' ass just started." He smirked before flipping me over and ramming himself inside of me.

Something was telling me what he said was nothing good; however, the way he was pumping his dick in and out of me had me not caring.

"Oouuu," I moaned as he slammed into me.

"You wanna be a whore? I'm gone fuck you like one," he growled, lifting one of my legs and rubbing my clit with his other hand. Hell, if this was what it took for him to fuck me like this, I should have been a whore. My body began to shake and unlike any other time, Blu didn't stop toying with my clit. He kept going, and I loved it.

My pussy was leaking like a broken faucet. All that could be heard were my moans and the sound of him digging in my guts. Blu let my legs down and pushed my back down so my arch could be perfect for him. He smacked both my ass cheeks before spreading them apart. The way that pill had me, I couldn't wait to get my hands on more. Blu was sliding his dick from my dripping center to my ass, and even that felt good to me. However, when he slid his dick into my ass, I screamed a little. It didn't hurt like it usually did, but I wasn't comfortable either.

"Shut the fuck up. You come in here wanting dick after you gave my pussy away, you gone get it any way I want to give it to you, bitch," he growled.

Blu reached under me and played with my pearl again, making me moan from the feeling I was now receiving. The shit felt so good I started throwing my ass back at him. Now his ass was in here howling to the moon. His body jerked and he shot his warm load into my ass. He pulled out and laid down, falling fast asleep while my ass laid there. I should have taken my money back, but I didn't. Blu had a side of him I didn't like. I saw how he would get angry and smack his bitches up. He never did it to me, and I didn't want to make him. Sliding my pants back on, I left out the same way I came. After taking another shower, I cleaned my whole house before I finally passed out on the couch.

19

MANNY

My boy was due to come home soon, and I knew his ass needed everything new. Of course, I had to hit the mall for him and grab him some clothes and shoes. It was about time he came back and took over the streets. The day he went to jail, Denver and I got together and moved all his work. The way sis bagged up the rest of his coke and weed surprised me. Her ass was always up under him, so it let me know she watched him a few times.

I swaggered into the sneaker store, and the first thing to catch my attention was this dark-skin girl. She wasn't dressed down, but her casual outfit was cute even though her pants looked a little worn down. It looked like she had just gotten off work by the little black shoes she had on, and I liked that. Walking up on her, I needed to see if she smelled good, and she did.

"Damn, back up," she sassed, turning around to face me.

"Your ass smells good as hell. This ass real?" I asked, reaching around her to touch it.

"You don't even know me to be touching me."

"I'm Emmanuel, you can call me Manny or daddy. I think I'll

like how daddy sounds rolling off your tongue, so let's go with that," I stated, stepping back into her personal space.

"Boy." She giggled while grabbing the shoes from the sales lady and sitting on the bench to try them on.

The moment she moved away from me, I frowned. For some reason, I wanted her ass close. It was almost like I craved her. Walking to the wall, I picked up five pair of sneakers I liked and told the lady what size to get. When I looked over, ole girl was looking dead at me with those brown eyes. She looked tired and sad, like life was beating her up. For some reason, my dumb ass wanted to help her. When she stood up and her ass got to jiggling with each step that she took, my dick stood at attention. She had a slight gap in between her thick thighs that I wanted to put my face in. I wanted her in the worst way. Walking up on her again, I placed my dick right on her soft ass.

"All those boxes right there and these too," I told the lady to ring all the stuff up so I could pay.

"You don't have to pay for my stuff, I got it. Why you look so familiar?" she said, looking over her shoulder at me. The way she kept staring was as if she was trying to figure if she knew me from somewhere, or maybe I was high and tripping.

"You don't know me, ma. If we knew each other, I would already be giving you daily doses of this dope dick. Give me yo' phone, though," I told her after I paid and handed her, her bag.

She took her phone out and handed it to me. I quickly dialed my number from her phone, handing it back after my phone rang. She looked at me like I was crazy, and I wanted to tell her I was but decided against it. While she stood there, I walked out the store without even saying bye. If she knew any better, she would call my ass so I could play my part in her life. If she decided to fuck with me, I wouldn't only be placing good dick in her life but a good life overall. Once I made it to my car, I had to laugh at myself. I hadn't even gotten her name. Shrugging it off, I pulled off and headed to the spot I had grabbed Zamir. Denver had decorated it and even had a key. I was sure he was gone be mad about it once he found out she was messing with this lame ass dude she met in college. But that ain't my story to tell, so when she wanted to, she would.

Denver was into the streets but green to the beef we had because before she could get a whiff of it, it would be handled. I had used the money we got from the work and got us a trap house. Instead of it being a bando like the other spots, I had moved one of the functional crackheads in. The bitch had one time to let the house get fucked up and she was out. The lady wasn't even allowed to get high in there, and she had to keep her job. I did that so it wouldn't look suspicious to the cops with us running in and out of it. That was the spot we used to cook our shit up and bag it up. Nobody was to go in that house but us, which was why I had cameras set up around the whole outside of it. We also had another spot that was in all our names. That's where we held meetings, got shipments, and did our dirty work. This place was called Taylor's Funeral Home. Yup, you read that shit right. My dad bought it for us since the nigga who owned it had a bad brain tumor and nobody to pass it off to. My dad did business with him, and since his shit was getting worse, he sold it for a low price.

My dad got fifteen percent of the payments, and the niggas who worked there stayed because we raised their pay. While I kept beef away from Denver, her ass seemed to find any little reason to kill a nigga, just to remind the team that just because she was a female didn't mean she couldn't fuck with the best of them.

"Boy, get out your damn head. I had to track your phone to find you. I just watched the footage for Auntie's spot, and the boys just ran up in that bitch," she whispered.

My face instantly frowned up. I was sure they ain't get shit because we ain't leave shit there for them to get. What got me was how they were able to get a search warrant. I was sure they ass ain't have no probable cause. Only people ever went there was us, so it only made sense that they were looking into one of us, and I ain't done shit recently.

"I already know what you thinking and besides school, I been out the way. We ain't have no run-ins with the law, so that only means we need to call a team meeting, because either somebody got sloppy or somebody talking. We're switching shit up to move everything out the spot and put that shit somewhere else. I'll send a location for the meeting, and you better not be late," Denver called over her shoulder while we were walking back to our cars. I wasn't surprised when she jumped in her car and peeled off. Her ass was mad, and I had to get to the people before she got to killing muthafuckas for nothing. That girl was a damn wild card.

Sending my dad and mom a code yellow text, I was sure they knew what to do. They would have everything moved and in a safe spot. We made codes when they first found out what we were into, in case they ever had to step in. Hopping in my car, I grabbed my burner phone and sent a mass text for everyone to meet at one of the vacant stores in my dad's lot. That was the only empty space I could think of right now, and I wasn't gone lie like we had it all together. We were still young and wet behind the ears. Of course, my dad could have schooled us, but we wanted it straight out the mud. It took me twenty minutes to reach my destination, and I was glad to see everyone's cars. I went and opened the gate, hit the lights, and everyone piled in. Closing the gate back, we remained quiet until my dumb ass little sister came in through the back door. This girl had switched clothes and was now in a black leather trench coat with the matching boots and gloves. Her weave that was once sitting on her ass was now in a ponytail. She looked like a damn character off *The Matrix*. When she saw how I was looking at her, she burst out laughing.

"I came dressed for the part, mind your damn business." She walked past me and pulled her guns out from her sides.

The two Glock 19 Gen 5 nine millimeters were sexy as hell.

But leave it to her to have on all black with two gold guns. Only Denver thought of shit like that. Everyone sat still, not making a move. The room was silent besides the clacking of her heels.

"Y'all know I don't like being here with guns drawn. You know I love my team. I would be ready to ride front line and die for you niggas, and the loyalty should be the same. So, therefore, this is hard for me. I mean, killing one of y'all would be, but paying for your funeral and hugging the person closest to y'all wouldn't. Anybody has any clue as to why the NARCS went to Auntie's house? Today's Tuesday, so y'all know this the day we're usually there taking care of family," she said. This crazy bitch kept pacing the floor.

"In two years, we ain't have no problems, no run-ins with the law, but now shit ain't looking as if we can keep it that way. I don't like that, and when I don't like something I usually remove it permanently. Now, I will find out who and what is going on and when I do, I'm gone kill your whole family, that's if you don't speak up now." She licked her lips before sitting in the only seat.

Nobody spoke up, like I expected. Our team wasn't big, it was a good fourteen of us, and we had it that way for a reason. It would take a lot of money and calls to figure out what the fuck was going on and why, but I was willing to pay it.

"Look, everything gone be switched around. Shut everything down for the rest of the day, no corners or no shit like that. Don't take the same routes, and if you do decide to bust a trap house, visits only." I dismissed everyone before crazy lady got to shooting at shit.

Everyone quickly got out, leaving Denver and me. She tucked her guns and looked up at me. It was easy to tell she was frustrated. When we got into this, Denver swore she had everything figured out, and the moment she didn't or felt like she wasn't in full control, she would make shit shake. People swore at first I would be the crazy killer one, but boy were they wrong. I was more rational, I liked to think. I found ways to solve the problem without killing, unless it was needed. My sister couldn't say the same.

"Look, we gone have to ask Kilo for help." Honestly, I didn't want to, but that was the only way we could get in with his dirty cop and see what was going on.

"I know. Let me know the price and I got half. I have class tonight, so I'm out." She dapped me up and left out the same way she came. Denver's ass was still mad. I couldn't wait for my boy's return. We needed to get this crazy girl out the game, because I could already see she was enjoying it too much, and that little cry baby ass girl she used to be was upgraded into a thug.

✸ 20 ✸

DENVER

I had been working at a nursing home for about three weeks now, and I just received my first paycheck. I been getting money, but it was nothing like legal money. Over the last two years, Manny and I got it out the mud. We created a few enemies that were all sleeping peacefully or backed down once they found out Manny was in charge. Plus, we had a whole team of muthafuckas who were loyal to us. We thought Kilo would be a problem since people stopped copping from him and started copping from us; yet, that didn't happen. It was like God was protecting me from problems in the streets but not with my life, at first. Kilo went into business with my dad, opening a little strip with barber shops, hair salons, and nail shops and whatever else people wanted to rent a space for. I had seen well over a fifty thousand, and a lot of it was put up for Zamir. Everything was all good, except the fact I couldn't figure out why we were under the cops' radar.

My grandma was so proud of me and though I never said it, it meant the world to me that I could make her proud. She hated how I started to get money but loved that I didn't have any trouble. Most people saw Manny ass the boss, and I was cool with that. My goal was to be legit anyway. This was only temporary, even though giving up the street life completely was something I couldn't see myself really doing.

"Good job today, Denver, keep up the good work," my supervisor, Rhonda, said to me as I grabbed my bag. My ass was rushing out the door. I had to make it to my grandma's house to drop some money off to her and then go to my little apartment and change clothes. Yeah, that's right, a bitch finally had her own spot.

"Thank you."

Today was the day that Zamir was supposed to come home, and happy was an understatement of how I felt. Since it was his first offense, the judge was lenient on him. He would do the rest of his time on probation, and he also had to do community service. I got in my car that my dad had purchased me and drove to my second home. Just like always, the smell of dinner greeted me; however, my grandma didn't. Walking inside the kitchen and stealing a piece of chicken, I noticed the bathroom door was ajar.

"Grandma, where you at, lady?" I called out but received no answer.

Judging from the silence, I could automatically tell something was wrong. Today was Saturday and anyone who was anyone knew that my grandma would have her Aretha Franklin playing while she cleaned up. What she cleaned, I don't know, because her house was always spotless. The feeling in my stomach was letting me know that something was wrong or off. I walked around the house and didn't find her. The only place left to check was her garden that was so precious to her. My grandmother would sit out there for hours and drink her freshly squeezed lemonade after she watered her plants and everything else that needed to be done.

Opening the back door, I smiled at my grandma. I could see her long black hair, which was naturally gray, but she always had me dying it jet black for her. She was seated in her chair with her head tilted back.

Walking around the chair, I tapped her on her shoulder a few times, but she didn't respond. My grandma was a light sleeper. Tapping her a few more times, I began to panic.

"Grandma, Grandma. Get up." Knocking her glasses off, I could see her eyes were still closed and her mouth was slightly opened.

Touching her neck, I felt for a pulse but came up empty, causing me to let out a gut-wrenching scream. Running back inside the house, I desperately searched for my phone. Remembering it was in my back pocket, I pulled it out and dialed 911 while quickly heading back to her. Placing my phone on speaker and talking, I laid her on the ground and began chest compressions.

"Grandma, please. Please don't leave me. I need you, I need you. Grandma, get up. I can't do this without you," I cried while pushing on her chest.

The lady on the phone was coaching me to keep going, and I had no plans on stopping. My arms were growing tired, but I just knew I could pump life back into her. My knees were hurting but my heart was hurting worse. It was slowly becoming hard to breathe, and while the lady on the phone was screaming for me to stop, I couldn't. I kept going, someone grabbed at my arm, and I knocked them away and kept pushing. It was my job to do all I could to save her like she had done me years back.

"Ma'am, we can't do our job if you don't move out the way."

I finally looked up with glossy eyes to see the paramedics. My heart was pounding, and my head was spinning. My arms were still moving. I couldn't stop, my next push on her chest could be the one to start her heart back up.

"I can't stop, call my dad and brother," I barely got out.

The paramedic guy picked me up and pulled me away. I kicked and screamed for him to allow me back to her.

"Call it," the lady said.

"5:11 pm."

When they pulled out the white sheet, I completely lost it. I slowly crawled back over to her with the little energy I had left and laid down with her.

"Grandma, please wake up, please get up. Don't do this to me. Please get up, I love you. I know I don't be saying it, but I do. Come on, ma," I cried.

Snot was running down my nose and into my mouth, but I didn't care. Everything I had to live for they were telling me was dead, and not coming back. Numbness started to kick in while I lay on that ground, but my tears never stopped falling. Grabbing the phone off the ground, I dialed my brother's number.

"Yo, sis," he answered on the first ring like always.

"Grandma," I got out and began to cry again.

I started to breathe deeper and more rapidly. I gasped for air as my chest began to hurt.

"Calm down, ma'am. Calm down, you got to be strong right now." The lady rubbed my back.

Had I been able to breath, I would have showed the bitch just how strong I was by knocking her the fuck out.

"Get the oxygen mask," she said, and I could hear movement. A couple seconds later, a mask was placed over my head, and it felt a little easier to breathe.

I laid there looking up at the sky, wishing God would take me too. As of now, I saw no purpose in pursuing life. The two most important people to me were somewhere in the clouds looking down at me. I wanted to be with them, hear my granny yell at me about not having a glass of water when I first woke up, but a nice big, ice-cold cup of her orange juice that she needed for her meds. My daughter finally had someone to take care of her. Silent tears fell down my face and wet my ears.

"What the fuck happened? Grams, nah yo. That better not be my fucking grams underneath that sheet." I heard Manny but couldn't move. He called out for me, but it fell on deaf ears.

My mind was trying to process this as well as figure out what went wrong. She looked so peaceful while sitting in her favorite spot, yet the image was so damaging to me and wouldn't leave my head. My dad was the next voice I heard, and his cries only made me cry even harder, except while they yelled and screamed, no sound left my body. My voice was gone and all I could do was stare at the sky. My dad lifted me up and held me in his arms. I knew it was him because of the cologne he always wore.

Wrapping my arms around his neck, I placed my head on his shoulder and let out cries I didn't know I still had in me. When my baby died, you couldn't tell me that, that wasn't the last time I would cry like that, because now look at me. Manny came and sat down on the ground, laying his head on my lap while my stepmom rubbed my dad's shoulders. You would think in a moment like this I would feel all the love; however, I felt lonely. My heart was completely broken and there was no healing it. Of course, my grams and I had it out a lot and we didn't always see eye to eye. There were so many times I wanted to pick up and leave, yet those were the times I would hold on to the most because she cared. She genuinely cared for me. It wasn't about no money or anything, her heart and intentions were pure.

"Just do everything you promised her to do. Graduate college, get that dream job, and do the damn thing with it, baby girl. Don't let that crown tilt. As hard as it is for all of us, I can't seem to fathom what it's like for you. Baby, don't you go blank on us, don't go saying fuck the world, 'cause ya grams wasn't raising you like that." My bonus mom held my face in her hands, making me look her in the eye.

She was squatted down in front of me, and her hazel green eyes were dark brown. Her entire face was red and her long pretty hair was pulled into a ponytail. The usual hyper her was gone and replaced with someone who looked like she could break at any moment.

"I'm going to try, but I can't make no promises. I felt so empty right now," I replied.

When the coroner came in and began to place her body in the bag, everyone broke down but me. My cries were gone. I walked over and kissed her now cold body and stepped back. My dad was on his knees looking like he was praying, while Manny was trying to take her body back out of the bag.

"Don't fucking touch me," he barked at one of the coroner's people.

Manny had now lost his cool and was trying anything for them not to zip our grandma up in that black bag. The corner had the police come in and restrain him, and even they had a hard time controlling him. When I saw one officer place his hand on his gun while the others fought to get him on the ground, I ran over trying to get through them. I got in front of the one who reached and placed my hands in the air.

"Please, don't do that. We already must bury our grandma. He's just hurt, that's all. Give him a second to say goodbye and allow him to calm down." Even as I said that, Manny was still trying to break free.

The cops were struggling bad; however, you could tell they were not trying to use anything to cause Manny physical harm. However, this cop wasn't getting that picture. I stayed in front of him until my dad got a hold of Manny and pushed him into the house. The coroner was able to do their job and they did it quickly. I watched as they wheeled my grandmother out and placed her in the back of the coroner's van. When they closed the door, I sat down on the sidewalk and put my head in my hands.

"What I'm 'pose to do now?" I spoke to no one in particular.

"You keep going," my dad said, causing me to jump.

When he had come out there with me, I wasn't sure and didn't even care. He kept on talking, yet nothing he was saying was registering. All I wanted to do was curl up in a bed and get high until I couldn't anymore. Standing up and walking into the house, I went inside my room and grabbed the Ziploc bag of weed that Manny had dropped off a few days ago.

I rolled up four backwoods and sparked one up. My dad and Trish seemed to have smelled it because they came in my room and joined the smoke session. Manny never came in, and I had to guess he had left.

"I don't know what we gone do with that boy. He was already upset that they gave Zamir another four months until he's released, and then he gets smacked with this," my dad said, causing me to look up. Za coming home had completely slipped my mind for the last few hours, and now that he wasn't coming home, I wanted to know why. Knowing Za, when he found out about Grams passing, he would lose his shit and more than likely have time added to his sentence again.

"I'm going to go find him and talk to him." My stepmom blew a cloud of smoke out of her nose and mouth.

"Nah, leave him alone. Give him some space. He's not going to be accepting of anything we say, just like somebody else we know. Nothing can change this moment. We have to come together and stay together as a family. Grandma's not here no more and Denver, baby, you gone have to take on a big role in this family. God not putting all this on you for no reason. You're strong, and no matter how the storm comes, you can make it out of it," my dad said as he handed me the blunt.

They both kissed my forehead and left me in the room to smoke and soak in my thoughts until I passed out.

21

MANNY

My mind was all over the place and I was angry with the world. Not only did I just lose my grandma, my whole heart, but the cops had done a bust on our funeral home. Since we had already switched shit around, they didn't get anything. However, nobody was making money like we should have been. We were sitting on a lot of weight because I wasn't chancing someone being locked up.

"Bro, you fucked up the count again. I told you we should do this shit another time. Let one of the little niggas handle this. We got to focus on Grandma's shit!" I yelled at Denver.

Her being her, she stood up and knocked the whole fucking table over. I looked at her like she was stupid. Denver's ass was two seconds away from being choked up, and I would deal with whoever later.

"Who the fuck you talking to? If you shut the fuck up or sat the fuck down, I could think straight. You handle your job, and I will handle mine. You mad at me when your ass not even getting on the cop shit yet. You're looking for real suspect right now," she spat, and I gripped her ass up.

"Look, bitch, you got me fucked up. Don't ever disrespect me like that. I ain't ever been no fucking rat." I tossed her dumb ass across the room. She went crashing into the wall, and I ain't give one single fuck.

"What the fuck is going on?" my dad screamed as he ran into the room.

Denver got up with murder in her eyes. She slammed her gun down on the table and ran around my dad and punched me in my face. The bitter taste of blood filled my mouth. When I spit the blood on the floor, she went to swing again, and I choke slammed her ass right through the table.

"Enough, y'all are fucking siblings!" my dad yelled, pushing me back.

Denver laid there for a second before she got up and grabbed her gun. Yeah, she was on straight bullshit. If she shot me, she was getting shot back and that was on my momma.

"Put the fucking gun down. Now y'all gone put y'all pride aside and figure this shit out. My mom is gone, she's not coming the fuck back, and wasn't shit nobody could do. She went out peacefully. I know her ass rolling over in the morgue at you two dumb asses. Now y'all shit getting shaky, and that's what happens when you in the game. Y'all was so used to y'all shit going y'all way and feeling like everything was on lock. The moment a problem comes, you both fold under pressure. Shit happens, what matters is what the fuck y'all gone do about it. Now here I am, we supposed to be at the damn service in fifteen minutes, and I got to break up a damn kid fight." My dad's voice stayed calm.

"I hear you, Dad, but he got me fucked up. You think you about to just slam me around?" Denver huffed.

Standing there with my arms folded, I dared her to try me. I would never punch her, but I would slap the shit out of her. She had three more hits and I was gone Ike Turner her ass up in here. Denver sat down when she realized she wouldn't win this fight. Turning around, I kicked the chair over then flipped the table, breaking it in half. I could hear my dad telling Denver to leave out, but of course her hard-headed ass stayed put. She reminded me so much of my dad it was crazy.

"Bro, look, I'm sorry, okay. I'm feeling this shit just like you. I may not have known Grams like you, but she saved me, and for that she meant the world to me. Just like you, I hate that it feels like control is slipping from us. We don't have a clue what the hell is coming our way and why. Daddy's right, it's not gone work if we're clashing. We got a team behind us that needs us. We got mouths to feed. Let's just take a step back for a second and let them continue to work how they are working. Focus on Grandma and get her service out the way. We gone take three days to clear our heads and come back to the drawing board." Denver stuck her hand out for me to shake.

As much as I wanted to break her fucking hand off, I didn't. My ass slid down the wall and cried. I cried for myself, for my family, for my grandma. Never in my life had I gone this long without hearing her voice, and it was eating at me. She would know what to do in a moment like this. I wanted to sneak and leave her weed and even go over just to have breakfast. The last few weeks I hadn't been seeing her as much 'cause I was so focused on my street shit. She had been on my ass to come see her too, and the moment I did, she was laid out dead. The hardest part for me would be seeing my grandma in that casket. I felt arms wrap around me and knew it was Denver just by that fruity ass smell.

"Bro, we gone spark up the whole car ride. We gone be in that bitch fried, we not gone cry in there either. Grandma ain't even play that shit, and you know it. We gone be strong for each other. Come on, dawg, let's go," Denver said, wiping away her own tears.

We stood up and walked out together. Instead of being dressed in all black, we were in all white with a splash of lavender cause those were grandma's favorite colors. Climbing inside the family car, it was quiet at first. My mom didn't even smoke with us, but she handed over her weed with ease today. The entire ride to the funeral home we smoked quietly, nobody said nothing, and we were all in our own thoughts. I smiled at the long line of cars. The whole hood came out for my lady. Once the car stopped, we got out and walked inside as a family and took our seats. My grandma didn't want to be buried, so we were getting her cremated. I think that took a weight off my dad because he kept saying he couldn't watch his mother be put in the ground. My grandma had life insurance and a will, so I knew after this we had one more thing to do, and I would try and put this behind me.

"Today we won't cry but smile, for Ann Mae Taylor lived her life," the pastor started, and I blocked his ass out.

The entire time I sat there blanked out, until our cousin Mary got to singing. This lady knew she couldn't sing for shit, so when they gave two minutes for everybody to talk, I wasn't expecting that shit.

"Only God may know why," she sang, sounding like a wounded fucking raccoon.

Looking over at Denver, she had oversized shades on her face with her hand over her mouth. I could tell by the way her body shook she was laughing, and my mom was doing the same, while my dad's leg bounced and he looked like he wanted to snap her neck. He stood up and my mom grabbed his hand, but he snatched away and grabbed the mic.

"Enough of this shit, Mary. You do this at everybody's damn funeral. You know good and damn well God did not blessed your ass with no voice from outside the shower. Get your ass on," he snapped at her, handing the mic back to the pastor, who looked afraid. They wrapped up the service and we piled in our cars and went back to grandma's house. I hadn't stepped foot in there since the day she died, so I sat outside with a bottle of Henny and my weed. Looking up at the sky, I asked Grams to protect us and help us get through this time like only she would know how.

22

JUSTINE

"Fucckkkkkk," I screamed out as Manny ate me from behind. Since the day I stumbled upon him, I had been waiting for this moment. Even though it was only two days ago, it felt like forever. My body shook and I came in his mouth. Like a thirsty nigga, he came off as he slurped that shit right up.

He let me up, wiping his chin that was covered with my juices. Grabbing his fingers, I sucked them in my mouth before dropping to my knees. His dick was at least ten inches and thick as hell. My mouth was watering at the sight of it and honestly, I didn't even like sucking dick, but I was about to enjoy sucking his. Grabbing a hold of his monster, I made sure my mouth was really wet before I slurped him up. A bitch's tonsils were removed when I was younger, so the gag reflex was gone. I teased him a bit, licking around the tip and sucking on the head.

"Mm," he let out, and I knew I was gone have his ass gone because I was just getting started. Removing my hands, I pulled away, spit on it, then swallowed him whole. While his dick was down my throat, I stuck my tongue out and licked on his balls. Pulling up for air, I twisted my head while jerking him off with my hand.

"Fuck," he yelled out as his body got tense and he shot his load down my throat, which I happily swallowed. I was done sucking, though I kept on going, causing Manny to pull me up by my hair.

"You trying to make me fall in love?" he asked me, and I smirked.

Climbing on his lap, I straddled him, my clit was pulsating, and I wanted him bad. Manny stopped me before I could slide down on him and grabbed a condom from off my coffee table. Yeah, I brought the pack out since I knew his ass was coming over. He slid it on and looked at me.

"Do your thing, and you better ride this muthafucka right." He slapped my ass.

Grabbing his tool, I lined it at my dripping entrance and slid down on it. I had to take my time 'cause his shit was thick and long. I rocked my hips back and forth before rotating my hips in a circle. Manny's head fell back, so I took that time to lick his neck. Using the back of the couch, I got up on my feet and bounced up and down, making us both moan. Manny lifted his head and placed his mouth on one of my nipples while pinching the other. That shit felt so good I never wanted it to stop. I wanted this feeling forever. Manny pumped his body underneath mine, and we fell into a rhythm of our own. I reached my hand down and played with my clit as my muscles tightened on him.

"Oh god, daddy!" I screamed out. Manny had taken full control by hooking his arms underneath my legs and bouncing me while slamming into me. Manny laid us on the floor, keeping his arm hooked, and gave me deep, long strokes. I felt like his dick was coming through my throat. When I felt the vibrator on my clit, my whole body jumped. He was sexing me so good, and the vibrator added on.

"Ahh, shit!" I yelled.

"Keep them legs open, stop playing with me," Manny growled.

I did as he said and looked in his face. He was looking down at his dick going in and out of me. That man was concentrating while blessing me with his devil dick. Manny chewed on his bottom lip, looking like a sex symbol. That man swirled his hips and my body lifted like I was in an exorcism. I knew my face was ugly, so I covered it.

"Mannyyy," I called out to him as my body shook like I was convulsing. I squirted all over his stomach and hand, and he kept going, he kept fucking me.

"I can't take no more." I tried to run, and his ass flipped me over like I was a rag doll. He arched my back for me and slid back inside of me, delivering powerful strokes. I knew my voice was gone be gone.

"Throw that shit back." He slapped my ass, and I did, bouncing my ass on him. Reaching under us, I played with his balls while throwing my ass.

"Damn" he hissed, and I kept going until he bust his nut. We fell forward and he laid on my back for about five minutes before pulling out of me. He went to throw the condom away while I laid on the floor. I swear I couldn't feel my legs.

Manny came back over and sat on the couch. He sparked his weed back up, taking a long pull. His ass kicked his feet up and flicked through the channels, looking for something to watch. His stomach growled loud as hell, and he looked at me. Since he had fucked me silly, I got my clown ass up real slow just to make sure I wouldn't fall. Looking through my fridge, I grabbed the eggs, bacon, pancake mix, grits, and shrimp. Yeah, it was around nine at night, but breakfast was the fastest thing. I moved around the kitchen quietly, feeling like Yvette off *Baby Boy* when she said, "I'ma cook, I'ma clean."

It took me a good twenty minutes before I was bringing him a tray with his food lined up on it, and yes, I did the whole presentation thing. If he gave y'all some of what I just got, y'all would understand. Placing his food in front of him, I went to clean up so I could take a shower.

"You need anything else? I'm about to go take a shower," I asked him.

"Come here and eat with me." He pulled me on his lap and fed me some of his food. I ate with him, and the whole time we laughed and joked.

"I don't know why, but this shit with you feels different. I usually fuck bitches and leave. Ya vibe tonight was cool as hell. I can see myself being around you a whole lot. Plus, you know how to make breakfast, and that's my favorite." He smiled, showing me them pearly whites.

I ain't really have too much to say. I liked his ass too, but I was damaged goods and nobody could save me. I kissed his lips and got up. Grabbing the box of condoms, I took them to my room. Tossing them on the dresser, they fell all over the place. I would pick them up after I washed my ass. Jumping in the shower, I let the water run over my body. It was strange for me to finally have someone like me enough to want to sit around, besides Blu, and I kind of liked him back. With Blu, I just felt like I wanted him around because he always was. He was handsome in a way, I just didn't trust him. Washing my body twice, I stepped out the shower and wrapped myself in a towel. Making my way back into my room, I picked up the condoms and noticed something was off with the wrappers. Going through them, I realized each one had a bunch of tiny holes in them. I quickly thought back to Blu and how he always said he wanted a baby by me. I would tell his ass no all the time, because I wanted to be married and in love with my child's father, if I ever had one.

God, don't let this birth control fail me, I thought to myself as Manny came into the room. He looked at me with lust-filled eyes.

"Aye, I got to make a run. I'll be back, though, if that's cool with you," he said, and I nodded when I knew I shouldn't.

His ass could make me feel things I should not feel. I was used to being alone and sleeping alone. Hell, Blu never slept in my bed, and here I was saying okay to Manny. His phone rang and he answered it.

"Son." I heard that familiar voice, and it clicked why I swore I knew him. His dick was too good, and the feelings he gave me were too much to leave him alone. I just prayed I could keep this a secret. All I had to do was never let us get to the point I met his family, and I would be able to keep him and my extra income.

❧ 23 ❧

ZAMIR

Standing outside the gates of hell, I took in a breath of fresh air. I had a few moments in the day over the last two years where I got an hour of this, and now I was inhaling so hard my nose was burning. I hadn't maxed out my time, so I still had to walk three years off on probation. I was always a built nigga; however, I had gained a few pounds, putting me at a solid two hundred and fifty pounds, and it was all muscle. Jail had done my body good.

Looking around at all the cars, I didn't see my nigga, Manny. He had told me he would be in a newer white Impala, which I didn't see in the parking lot so far. I was praying like hell he ain't forget to come get me. A few minutes went by when an all-black Dodge Durango pulled up and stopped in front of me with windows heavily tinted. Acting off instinct, my hand went to my waist. I had to laugh at myself because there wasn't a shank or a gun there, and if whoever was here to take me out, I was sure they would succeed. Taking a step back as the door on the driver's side opened, I waited to see who it was and what was about to happen.

A big smile graced my face that I quickly replaced with a frown when I saw Denver's little ass. Her body was still very much the same. However, her hips had spread a little more. Hell, the small gap in between her legs was the same. Even with the slight frown that graced her face from the sun shining down on her, Denver still had my attention and was still the most beautiful girl in the world to me.

"Damn, the first time you see me in years, and you got a frown on your face. I should have left your big ass here," she shot as she came over to me.

Same ignorant ass little girl too, I thought to myself.

"Man, where my boy at?" I questioned, shaking my head.

"He had a business meeting he couldn't miss. So, I'm gone bring you to my house and get back to my online shopping. He gone swing by and get you when he's done."

Denver stepped into my space and my dick instantly bricked up. The dark-blue, distressed jeans she had on were hugging her like they were painted on, and her titties were sitting right in the top she was wearing. Her little shoes gave her extra height and she stopped right at my chest. I didn't know if it was the lack of pussy or the fact that she was beautiful that had me mesmerized. Licking my lips, I looked her over once more. I had to smirk when my eyes made it back to her face, because she was staring at my dick print, chewing on her bottom lip.

"Don't make me put him in ya life," I threatened, and she laughed.

I watched her walk back over to her car and climb in. I followed suit and wasn't surprised when I got inside. Her seats were black with hints of white, and it smelled fruity just like she always did. She never cared the name of the scent, and no particular one was her favorite. If it smelled fruity and good, she would wear it. This smell she was wearing had my dick getting harder by the second.

"Here." She reached over into the glove compartment and tossed me a stack of money and an all-black Glock .40.

"Don't never say I ain't gave you nothing."

I sat there counting the money while she drove around. The

window was down and the air was feeling good against my skin. She had handed me ten thousand dollars in all twenties. I knew the kind of job she had and knew that she either saved this shit or she was doing extra work on the side.

"How you get this?"

"Don't worry about that, just know it's rightfully yours. Thank you for punching that nigga for me. I wish I could have given you more." She looked over and smiled at me.

"This enough. Where we headed? I need a cut, a shower, and some clean clothes. A nigga looking real fucked up right now."

"I told you to my house until Manny comes to get you. If only you could see what I saw," Denver mumbled the last part, but I heard her.

Biting on my bottom lip, my mouth slowly formed into a smile. This girl was tempting me, and if that pussy was as good as I imagined, then I wanted, no, needed some of that gushy shit. About twenty minutes later, we pulled up to a row house and she got out. She stepped out and I followed her up the steps. I watched her use a key and unlock the door. It was dark as hell when we walked inside due to the blackout curtains that hung on the big ass window. Denver flicked the lights on, and I knew it was her house. On the wall sat a big photo of her and Grams with other small photos surrounding it. Instead of the fruity smell, it smelled like bleach and cleaning stuff, letting me know she had just cleaned up.

"Make yourself at home. Manny gone be by to pick you up and take you to your place. I'm going to go lay down, finish online shopping, and enjoy my day off. You can use the guest room to clean up. Your clothes are in there as well as towels and all that shit."

When she went up the steps, my eyes followed her. I walked around the house before going up the steps and finding the guest room, which was the only door left open. I grabbed the clothes and headed in the bathroom and took a shower. I washed my body about three times before stepping out. After I dried off, I threw on an all-black Dickies set with the tan Timberland boots. Walking out the room, I went and knocked on Denver's door. Her house was nice, but I needed to know when Manny was coming. Being stuck in the house was the last thing I wanted to do.

Denver was talking on the phone and giggling. I opened the door, and she was laid across the bed with the phone to her ear while on her laptop. She looked up at me and stopped talking. The way her lustful gaze traveled my body, I knew a nigga looked good. Whoever she was on the phone with must have been calling her name, because she snapped out of it.

"Yeah, babe?" she said while we locked eyes.

She ended the call with an "I love you too." That damn near made me yoke her ass up. Wasn't no way she loved this babe person when the last time we talked, she promised to only love me. Shit, I didn't even think I could love a girl until I loved her ass, and here she was giving the love she was only supposed to have for me to someone else.

"You love him?" I had to ask. My heart rate picked up when she opened her mouth and closed it.

"Do you fucking love him, Denver?" I asked more sternly.

She nodded her head yes, and I turned on my heels and stormed out of her room, slamming the door behind me. How could she love someone when she promised to wait for me? I knew almost six years was a long time, but that's why she was free to do what she wanted. However, her loving someone wasn't a part of the plan. Plus, that time was knocked down and I only did two year. She hadn't even known the pussy that long.

"Zamir, why the fuck you won't just listen to me, damn." Denver grabbed my arm and pulled it so I could face her.

Turning towards her, I stared down at her little ass with the meanest mug I could muster up on my face.

"Fuck you want me to listen to, huh? You must have bumped your big ass head if you think for one second I want to hear about you loving this man. I get it, and I know what's up. I'm gone go find me a bitch to love too. We can be cool, you my dawg forever, and I always got you, but clearly this ain't what it was supposed to be." I pointed between us.

"Really? Find a bitch to love? Zamir, no bitch in this world gone love you like I do, nor hold you down like I did, and I can bet my life and yours on that. But go ahead and find her. Every time you slide up in that bitch, you gone wish it was me," she snapped like she had the right to be mad.

Laughing at her, I turned and headed down the steps. Wasn't no way I was gone be sitting around waiting for her man to come home, then I would be wrong if I knocked his ass out. I opened the front door, and she reached around me and pushed it closed. Now, due to our size difference, I could have easily overpowered her and tossed her little ass somewhere and bounced, yet I would never put my hands on her. Rubbing my hands over my face, I tried to calm myself down. She was about two seconds from me gripping her the fuck up and snapping the fuck out.

"You gone listen to me, and when I'm done, you can walk your overly huge ass out here if you want to." She folded her arms over her chest like she was doing something.

"Look, I'm not in love with him. But yes, I do love him, I think anyway. He is innocent and saving himself for marriage, so we not even having sex. I love that he's a momma's boy and that he listens and deeply cares for me. We go on dates and all that good stuff, and after a year of that, of course I grew love for him. Zamir, you know how I feel about you, yet we know how you are. You so caught up on my brother not wanting us to be together or what would happen to y'all friendship if you hurt me, that you place me on the back burner. Zamir, how long you expect me to deal with that? It's either you all in or you not. We not teenagers sneaking around to be in each other's presence no more. I'm a grown ass woman with my own shit, in college, and have a nice job," she told me.

"I don't give a fuck about none of that. You love that man, so continue to do so," I barked. That was all I cared about. Fuck they dates, the nigga whose nut sack he came swimming from, the bitch that pushed him out, and everything else she said. My heart was aching, and I wanted to make that muthafucka stop.

Moving her to the side, I walked out the door and slammed it with so much force. My ass was trying to break it or at least take the doorknob with me. This time she didn't come outside, and I was grateful for that. I sat on the porch trying to wipe away images of her kissing him and loving him. The way she said it, I knew she meant it, and that's what hurt me more. I didn't regret going to jail for her because I knew that it was the right thing for me to do, knock that cop the fuck out. I could easily do the time like I did. Manny pulled up and didn't even have to get out of the car. I jumped up and climbed in before he could open his door.

"Fuck happened with y'all?" he asked, probably judging by the mean mug I couldn't wash off my face.

"Ain't shit I'm about to dwell on. Let's just go to the barber-shop and whatever else you want to do, so I can find myself balls deep in a bitch's throat to relieve this stress."

"You must know about ole boy then." He laughed.

Frowning at him, I kept my mouth shut, knowing his ass would keep on going if I said anything. A nigga was home, and the last thing I was about to do was stress. Shit, I was about to do everything I wanted with no cares in the world. Just because I deserved to.

24

DENVER

"Baby, what's wrong?" Joseph asked me.

My mind was consumed on the fact it had been a week since Zamir and I had our conversation, and it hurt like hell that I wasn't even allowed to attend his welcome home party. He had security turn my ass right around at the door. I had half a mind to go past them and punch him in his face, but I didn't. More than anything, we could have kept our friendship, but he was acting like he didn't want any of it.

"Babe, do you hear me? What's going on?" Joseph shot question after question. Letting out a deep sigh, I focused in on his dark-brown skin, which reminded me more of rich dark chocolate. Even with his few pimples on his face he was still fine. His teeth were pearly white and straight thanks to the braces he had just gotten removed. Joseph kept his hair cut low with a few waves in it. He fixed his gaze on me, and I shifted in my chair uncomfortably. Here I was with this man who I knew loved me outside of my pussy, and I had another man on my mind.

"Nothing much. I just been thinking I know you want to wait for marriage to have sex, but we really can't even do oral?"

"No, I've done enough with us kissing. It is important to me and my family to do so. Heck, I would have been married you, but something's holding you back from that. My mother would probably have a heart attack if she knew that I even used my fingers on you and allowed you to use yours on me," he replied while taking a sip of his Bloody Mary drink.

We were on one of our many dates, and while I sipped on a nice cool glass of champagne, he preferred tomato juice. His mother was a cold hoe and he thought nothing of it because she was a deacon's wife. Hell, everybody knew church women be the freakiest ones. Joseph had a nice-sized dick, and I was dying to get a taste of it. No matter how many times I had him melting in my hand, he wouldn't let me sit on it. At this point, I was desperate for dick because my toy wasn't doing it for me anymore.

"That's what's been bothering you, sweet pea?"

I shook my head while trying to hold in my laughter. He was so perfect and far from what I was used to. That's the reason I was with him, yet all the pet names he gave were hilarious to me. I was so used to being called someone's bitch or their wifey that I still wasn't used to this. I often answered him and smiled, knowing that this was how a man should treat me. Even if I hated the fact that I could walk all over him, and if anything ever went down, I would be the one to protect us both while he would be the one ready to call the cops. Joseph knew nothing about the life I lived outside of college. He thought I was this smart girl who came from a family of money. He had seen me counting money one time, and I lied and sad my daddy gave me an allowance. However, that shit was straight drug money.

"Joe, that's one of the main things bothering me. I'm trying to hold off on sex, but it's getting harder by the day. I want to sit on your face and then taste my juices on your lips," I spoke lowly, running my tongue over my lips.

"Woah, calm down. I don't know about all those things, and why would you want to taste yourself? Is this what people are doing? I thought sex was completely different. I'm not too sure on putting my mouth where someone pees." He frowned his face in disgust.

I sat back in my chair and let out a breath. I wasn't sure how much longer I would be able to survive this torture. The thought of cheating crossed my mind for the thousandth time in this relationship. This had to be the reason guys cheated when girls held out on them. I was being deprived of dick and my toys were not it. The feel of a man holding me while giving me deep strokes was what I wanted and needed. We continued eating until someone bumped into our table.

"Oh, excuse me."

I looked up at the tall, chocolate, pretty girl. Her body was flawless. I damn near spilled my drink when I locked eyes with the person holding her hand, and then knew the bump to the table wasn't too much of an accident.

"Damn, what's good, Denver." Zamir smirked.

"Hello, how are you this evening?" I replied, and he looked at me like I had grown two heads.

"Nah, you got that fake ass proper voice on for your dude. What's good, ole boy," Zamir greeted Joseph, who looked scared as hell.

"Let me holla at you right quick." Zamir grabbed my hand and pulled me from the table.

I tried to snatch away, but he pushed my ass towards the bathroom, locking us inside. He looked me over, biting his bottom lip, and I swear my dumb ass came on myself. He looked into my eyes, running his tongue over his bottom lip real slow.

Yep, I came, I thought to myself. This man had me pinned against the door, and we were so close I could feel his heart beating. He grabbed me by my neck and gave my lips a small peck.

"Za, we have people out there," I whispered, trying to convince him and myself to stop.

"So what, they can fucking wait." My pussy was dripping just by the authority he had in his voice.

Zamir placed his lips back on mine and this time, I kissed

him back. His hands cuffed my ass and he slowly massaged it while we fought for dominance in the kiss. His ass won when he bit my bottom lip.

"Za," I moaned out, and this man traveled his kisses from my lips to my neck then to my ear, where he sucked on my earlobe. I could feel his hard dick pressed into my stomach and I wanted it bad. Za lifted me up and sat me on the counter. He lowered himself down and lifted my dress up around my waist. That man moved my panties to the side and kissed my lower lips. My head fell back against the mirror as he licked and sucked my clit into his mouth. Zamir grabbed my ass and pulled me closer, burying his face in my shit.

"Oh god, I missed you so much," I cried out.

He slid a finger inside of me and my back arched. Grabbing the back of his head, I grinded into his face until I was coming all over it. Za stood to his feet, wiped his mouth with the back of his hand, and walked over to grab some paper towels. He wet one and wiped his mouth the best he could. I wanted him so bad, and it felt so right. The way my pussy was tingling made me want more of him, and if Joseph's ass didn't break some off, I was gone be climbing Za's big ass and letting him bust this pussy right open.

"We need to talk," I told him.

"You know how to find me," he said before pecking my lips and leaving my ass sitting on the counter looking stupid.

🐾 25 🐾

JUSTINE

I knew just how much of a fucked-up individual I was in this moment. I was sitting here with the husband of the same lady I had been sneaking and seeing. He was wining and dining me with those bubbly eyes. The entire time he talked about what we could be, I was thinking about his son. Yeah, I knew, his ass showed me a picture of him. While explaining to me how proud he was of him, he also told me about his daughter. He didn't need to know that I was messing with him, just like he didn't want his wife to know he had been sending me money and texting me about how much he wanted to taste my pussy again. If only he knew how much his wife was saying the same thing. So, before he brought me out shopping, I let him lick me from head to ankle. The more he talked, the more I realized that he didn't really like me that much; he liked the thrill of things. Just like his wife Trish's ass was just trying to have fun like she was twenty-one again and have a friend that she had complete access to. We sat side by side with each other in the booth, while he laughed, talking about his son. Hell, the more he mentioned him the more I wanted to see him, so I shot him a text to come see me tonight. Since Manny had blessed me with that dick, I hadn't fucked Blu, and he was pissed. Whenever I was home, my ass pretended not to be because he would bang on my door calling me all kinds of hoes and tell me he was going to ruin my new nigga. He ain't even know who he was, so that was the least of my concerns.

"My wife looking for me, her ass back home early. Don't forget to send my video to my wife so she can watch it with me." He pulled me to him and kissed me on the lips.

I watched his dick print when he stood up. Maurice dropped a stack of money on the table and walked off. After ordering my Uber, I grabbed the money placed a hundred-dollar bill on the table for the food and left out. Between him and his son blowing my back out, I wasn't sure how my pussy stayed tight. Having the three of them was a major blessing. I finally had enough money to buy me a car. Uber was getting old, and I was happy as hell to finally be able to go purchase some shit I could call my own, even if it came from me being a hoe. I didn't even have a license, but I would get one, after I got my car though.

Stepping into my house, I kicked my shoes off and walked dead smack into a slap. Falling to the floor, I quickly jumped up to my feet and started swinging blindly on my intruder.

"Bitch, you out here being a hoe and I can't even get a cut? You fucking people in here, and now I can't even get no pussy!" Blu yelled as we went at it.

Blu gripped me by my throat and slammed me onto the couch. He lifted my dress, and I swore this would be the last time I ever wore one. Grabbing his face, I clawed at it, making him wince in pain. Blu slapped my ass so hard I was shocked. It was as if he was trying to literally slap my head off. He quickly pulled his cuffs off his side and handcuffed me. Kicking my feet was now the only thing to help myself, so that's what I did, kicked and screamed, hoping one of these damn neighbors heard me. When he pulled his gun out and placed it inside of my mouth to muffle my screams, I grew scared. In a way, I wanted him to pull the trigger. He was violating me in the worst way. Blu pulled his dick out and forcefully pushed inside of me, and since

I wasn't horny, it felt like he was about to start a fire. He licked his hand, rubbed my pussy, then spit on his dick before sliding back inside of me. Crying wasn't helping me, so I laid there and just took it until he came.

"You know I love you, right? I don't want to lose you for nothing. That's my pussy, and you giving it away and not giving me money for it is wrong. I will tell you what, the family you're fucking has more than enough money legally and illegally. I've been watching you, so either give me a cut of what they're giving you, or I'll have your ass arrested for prostitution and them down for their drugs," he threatened.

Nodding my head, I agreed with him. If I had to give his ass two hundred dollars to leave me alone, I would. Now more than ever, moving was a priority. I couldn't be here, knowing he was watching me and had access to my place. The moment I moved out of here, I was changing everything, even how I dressed and looked, to get him away from me. What was bothering me most was I didn't know if I should warn Manny or not. Things like this usually didn't go well, so keeping my mouth shut may just be the best idea. Blu climbed off me then proceeded to uncuff my hands. He never put his gun away, making me stay in my spot until he was out the door. The moment my front door slammed, I ran into the bathroom and locked the door. Kneeling over the toilet seat, I vomited up everything I ate today. I threw up until I was dry heaving. The salty taste of snot mixed with my tears was in my mouth, and I didn't care.

Turning the shower on, I didn't wait until it heated up. I climbed inside of it and scrubbed my body clean. If I were light skin, my skin would have been red from the way I was scrubbing. When my shower curtains flung open, I almost jumped out of the tub and my heart was pounding.

"Why you leave your door un—" Manny stopped midsentence and looked at my face. He grabbed my face and turned me to him.

"Fuck is you crying for? What's up, talk to me," he said while sitting his gun on the toilet seat. He pulled his watch off, kicked his shoes off, and climbed in the shower with me fully clothed. Manny held me tight while I cried on his chest. I loved that he didn't continue to ask questions, he just held me tight. We stayed like that until the water ran cold. Manny stepped out, grabbed my towel, and handed it to me. He peeled his now soaking wet clothes off and wrapped a towel around his waist. Grabbing his clothes, I put them in the dryer while he grabbed his gun. Manny was showing me the perfect example of taking his gun everywhere with him.

"I, he, he..." I tried to get out, but only began to cry again.

"Shhh, it's okay. I'm here, and any time you need me, call me. I will come. Whatever you need, I got you." He kissed the side of my head. For some reason, I felt safe in his arms. I just couldn't form the words to tell him what was going on. So, I laid on his chest and cried myself to sleep.

✤ 26 ✤

ZAMIR

Denver's ass was supposed to be at my house twenty minutes ago, and it was pissing me off. I knew she was at her little boyfriend's event, but my time was precious. I was ready to get back to the money. My phone chimed, indicating I had a text.

3:22 pm
Heartbreaker: On my way!

3:23 pm
Me: Your dumb ass been 'posed to be here. I got shit to do and my bitch trying to slide. Hurry up, bald head.

3:24 pm
Heartbreaker: Keep playing with me like you don't love your life.

Denver's ass was always threatening me. She swore up and down she could beat me or that she would kill me if I ever made her feel like a girl had my heart. Whole time she was out here playing with fire. Grabbing the bottle of Hennessy off my table, I poured me a drink and waited for her to come. A few minutes went by, and I heard my front door open. Grabbing my gun from my waist, I aimed it at the walkway. This bald ass little girl walked in smiling, looking good as hell. Licking my lips, my eyes traveled over her body. Instead of the burgundy looking color she usually had, her weave was jet black and straight as hell with the perfect part in the middle. She had on a tight ass pair of white shorts and a black v-neck Polo T-shirt. On her feet were a pair of Jordans, and she sported a book bag today instead of one of those big ass pocketbooks she be having.

"Why the fuck you got a key?" I asked her. She had to have one since I always locked my doors.

"'Cause I do, now let's talk business." She walked over to me and tossed me the book bag.

I caught it with ease and smiled. This was the same book bag I had when I got locked up that I kept my money in. Instead of it being light, it was heavy. Looking over at her, I waited for her to talk.

"It's about thirty thousand in there, that's all you. Manny and I are in business together, but since you're home, I'm stepping down and handing my spot over to you. For two years we built a solid team, or what I thought was solid. I'm not gone step all the way down right now because we are having some trouble with the police, and I'm not sure why. It would be fucked up for me to put you in a position like that again. My whole reason for even being in the game is to make sure I could upgrade your ass like you had done me. Now it's time for me to focus completely on school and myself. I will still cook up the work and bag it for y'all, but I need to get paid for that. We can discuss that and everything else when my brother gets here," she spoke confidently.

My ass was proud of her. My bitch was out here putting in work for me. I loved her even more for that shit. Standing to my feet, I walked into her personal space and pulled her into a hug, kissing all over her face and cuffing her juicy ass.

"Thank you, you don't know how much this shit means to me," I whispered, licking her ear.

I would give that whole book bag up and get it from the mud if it meant I could have her ass. She was all I ever wanted. Denver pecked my lips then walked into the kitchen to help herself to whatever. Grabbing my phone, I sat on the couch and texted a few bitches back.

"What are you doing? You know it's no phones when I'm around. Ain't shit changed, it's me and you," she yelled.

"I'm looking for a girl since my heart got snatched from me," I joked.

Denver walked up on me with a frown. She climbed in my lap and looked me in my face.

"You are killing me," she uttered.

"Good, because if you don't drop that nigga soon, I'm gone kill him too. Y'all gone be dead together." I grabbed her by the throat and applied light pressure before kissing her lips. She slipped her tongue into my mouth, and my dick instantly bricked up.

"Let me eat," I said in between kisses. Denver smirked and stood up off me. She slid her shorts and panties off real slow, and I made her bend her ass over right there and touch her toes while I kept my seat on the couch. I licked her from her ass crack to that dripping wet box, making her body shiver. Taking my time, I kissed both her cheeks before spreading them and sucking her clit into my mouth.

"Mmmhhh," she moaned out. Twisting my tongue in and out her hole, I rubbed her clit with one finger while using my other hand to ease my thumb in her ass.

"Oohhh, I'm 'bouta cum," she let out, grinding her pussy into my face. I moved my fingers faster as her juices squirted all over my face. Her phone began ringing, and looking over at the screen, I dared her to answer it.

She smirked at me before picking it up.

"Hey, baby." She smiled into the phone. Since she was still in the same position, I whipped my dick out and rubbed it against her folds, making her bite her bottom lip. Once the tip of my dick was wet, I slid inside of her inch by inch.

"Fuck," I growled lowly.

"Hmmmm? I told you, I'd be—aghhh," she tried to talk, but I finally eased my way all the way in her.

I squeezed her ass cheeks while giving her slow, deep strokes. Lifting one of her legs, I placed it on the table and grabbed a handful of her weave. Her shit was so tight and creamy, I just knew I was gone be in it all the time. There was no way I was giving this shit up. Her ass was really stuck with me now.

"Let me call you back!" she screamed, hanging up the phone. Her hands clenched the phone while I picked up the pace, giving her death strokes. She threw her ass back at me, making the shit feel even better. Not wanting to moan like a bitch, I bent forward, kissing and licking up and down her spine. Picking her up, I slid out of her and laid her on her back. Bending down, I placed her legs over my shoulders before sliding back inside of her. I held on to her legs, pushing them as far back as they could go, and she could feel every bit of these eleven inches.

"I love you so much, Zamir," she cried as I pumped inside of her.

Leaning down, we shared a sloppy kiss. Placing my hand on her throat, I squeezed, applying some pressure but not enough to where she couldn't breathe. Each time I pumped inside of her I made sure to go deeper. I was trying to fuck her silly since she wanted to play with me.

"I can't take no more, daddy!" She screamed as her body jerked and she creamed all over my dick.

"You ain't got no choice," I told her as I kept up my pace. All that was heard were the sounds of her moaning my name and our skin slapping. I gripped her legs and held them tight, digging my fingers in them. I shot my seeds deep inside of her then pulled out.

"You really didn't just do that," she said, out of breath.

"That's on you. Shouldn't have smirked at me." I stood up and tucked my dick back in my pants.

Denver stood up and grabbed her shorts and panties. Her ass tried to walk off with an attitude. Her little ass was walking with a limp instead. I went into the guest bathroom since she went in mine, to brush my teeth and wash my face and hands. I wiped my dick off and tucked it back just in enough time to hear Manny's ass yelling for me.

I came out of the bathroom just as Denver came from the other direction. Her hair wasn't perfect like it was when she walked in, but I could tell she tried to fix it. Manny looked between the both of us before laughing.

"Den, you grown now, so I ain't gone scold you. You're playing with fire, and both you niggas know it. Y'all can mix y'all pleasure with business, but don't let that shit interfere with my money," Manny said sternly.

I ignored everything he just said. Now that I had the pussy, wasn't no way I wasn't getting that shit whenever I wanted. On top of that, I knew nobody was sliding in it but me, and that made me want it even more.

"Now that you here, we can get down to what y'all wanted me to know. Bald head filled me in for the most part. I just want to know when I start and where everything's located. I need to grab another wheel too, can't be doing business in my personal cars."

27

MANNY

I bobbed my head to the music and drove through the hood, occasionally letting my window down, and Za and I would hold a conversation with people from the neighborhood. I was showing him the blocks we had people hustling on and the spots we used for packages, and whatever else he need to know about. My boy was finally home and was gone run the streets with me both legally and illegally.

"I don't think Denver wants to hand over her position, and I'm cool with that as long as I'm getting to the money as well," Za said, but my mind was on Justine and what happened to her.

I kept trying to tell myself to stay away from her. She clearly didn't trust me enough to let me help her, but my ass kept finding myself in her bed. I knew she had something going on with somebody else because her phone was always going off and she would ignore it. I wasn't even mad at her about shit like that because she wasn't my bitch, and I was still doing me. That didn't mean I didn't feel a bit jealous each time. We pulled up to the last spot and got out of the car.

"Fuck we doing at a funeral home?" Za said, grabbing his gun and cocking it.

"Boy, put that shit up. This the spot where we were holding

everything. As of now, we not, because for some reason the cops trying to make a bust on us. We own this muthafucka. We can put your name on shit now that you home. No more slanging on the streets, though. We worked hard for two years so you wouldn't have to come back and do no shit like that. Focus on doing something you love to do that's legit. We gone let them make the illegal money for us and step in when we have to. We ain't no big-time drug dealers or none of that shit, and that was never our goals. We are respected and have enough money to get us by and enough to open some shit up," I told him.

"I hear you, I just don't feel like y'all handing me this shit is cool. Niggas gone be hot about that, and I want to do less killing and more working. Plus, I ain't ever been that dude. I'm gone put work in too. Now I ain't got to play the blocks if that helps y'all, but I'm getting in the lab and I'm gone do some work too." He shrugged, not giving a fuck about what I just said.

"Cool, just don't forget to find you some legit shit to do." It wasn't no point in arguing with him.

"I'ma start a cleaning company and a moving company. I'm gone hire felons too, but if they fuck up, I'm gone shoot them. Won't be messing my name up." He laughed.

We walked into the building and into the basement. Za turned and went back up the steps and out the door, and I had to laugh. This man killed a lot of people but didn't fuck with dead bodies at all.

"Bro, all of them dead niggas should be in freezers or some shit. I ain't coming back in here," he yelled down the steps.

The people who were down their putting up the bodies we had just received started laughing. I jogged up the steps and went to find Za, who was across the street sitting on the bus stop.

"You just gone let me walk into that spot. They had dead dick and pussy swinging in there. The ghosts probably in there laughing at me. You should have warned me. I don't fuck with the dead, I can't kill them," he said, wiping the sweat from his forehead.

"Man, stop bitching. Them dead people ain't worried about you. Come on." I went to my car and jumped in.

Za waited a while before he got in the car, and I drove off. His ass was getting dropped off so I could go slide in some cheeks.

"Aye, you know Denver's old best friend's name was Justine. It's crazy how you done found you a bitch with the same name," he said, reminding me of Denver's friend name.

"Yeah, but this one from Jersey not Philly. Her vibe is crazy, so if shit go good with her, I can link them, and they probably would be cool as hell. But then again, Denver don't like nobody." I laughed. My sister had become selfish with me. So, her feeling like she had to share me with a female was a no go. I knew she mainly did the shit because of how I was with her and Za when we were younger.

"That's good you got somebody that make you want them off their vibes alone. The only person that ever made me feel like that makes me want to shoot her and everybody at the same time. I can't say her little ass heartless 'cause she not. Ole girl know what she's doing though, which is why I'm trying to keep my cool. I ain't gone lie though, if she ain't have me hooked before, I'm definitely hooked now." Za smirked.

My ass was glad we pulled up to his spot, because I didn't want to hear that shit about my sister. After kicking his ass out, I headed straight to see Justine. The room she was staying in sort of looked like an apartment with two rooms. This hotel was a nice getaway, and I was gone use it when needed. Using the key to let myself in, I saw Justine in the kitchen cooking something that smelled good as fuck. Her hair was up in one of those messy buns. She had on a pair of boxers that hugged her ass like a second skin and a sports bra with fuzzy socks on. To me, she looked beautiful. I loved this look on her more than anything else. Her hips had spread a little and her ass grew. Licking my lips, I walked up on her and wrapped my arms around her.

"You're getting thicker. All you needed was my dick to really have that ass sitting right." I kissed her cheek.

Looking over her shoulder, I saw she was making some popcorn chicken, mashed potatoes, gravy, and corn. My stomach growled just from the smell. Justine turned her head and gave me a quick kiss on the lips.

"I'm almost done, everything goes into one bowl. I saw it on Instagram and wanted it," she spoke.

"Bet, I'm about to roll up. You need me to do anything?" I asked her.

"Nah, just smoke with me. Oh, and maybe rub my scalp like you be doing. That shit feels good. You staying here, or you leaving?" she questioned while cutting the stove off and rinsing bowls before sitting them on the counter.

Shrugging my shoulders, I went into the room she slept in. I didn't too much understand why she had a whole damn apartment but would rather be in this damn hotel. Each time I brought it up, she would cry so hard that I would just leave it alone. Pulling my sneakers and jeans off, I sat on the bed and rolled up so we could smoke twice. Just as I finished up, Justine walked in the room with the food. While she sat it down, I went and got us both something to drink before climbing in bed with her. We smoked, ate, and then smoked again before I found myself rubbing my fingers through her hair while we watched a movie. I felt content in this moment, and I wouldn't mind it becoming a permanent part of my life.

✵ 28 ✵

DENVER

Walking into Joseph's mom's backyard, I got the surprise of my life. Her ass was bent over the table snorting a line while her husband lit his bowl. Had Joseph not told me to meet him there to take them out for dinner, I would have missed this shit. It was amusing to me to watch these people who judged everyone do this shit. Pulling out my phone, I got a little video just in case shit with them ever hit the fan. They loved their image more than anything in the world. At first, I was so shocked at what they were doing I couldn't even say anything.

Placing my phone in my pocket, I decided to speak. "Well, hello, Mr. and Mrs. Wells." I called them by their last name because that's what they told me to.

That lady almost jumped out of her skin. She quickly wiped her nose and tried to hide her shit underneath the flowerpot she had on the table. Shaking my head, I took a seat. The smell didn't bother me. Hell, I was used to it.

"Oh, don't mind me, finish doing you. Let's just say you better not ever open your mouth to call me another name in the book to your son, because I'm sure your family doesn't know you like to get high as a kite. Oh, and if you ever looking for some, hit me up. This could be our little secret." I dropped a small bag I had in my pocket on the table and walked back in the house.

My ass sat on the couch and waited for everyone to arrive. They stayed in the backyard, and I'm sure it was to finish their shit. About an hour went by before Joseph walked in with a girl I had never seen before. They both were smiling like kids on Christmas, and it was cute. What was mine was mine, though, and a bitch like me ain't share unless I wanted to, and this wasn't the case.

"Hey, Denver," Joseph greeted me, pulling me into a hug.

Looking at him, I tried to read him. Oh, he was on to something, because his ass called me by my first name. Usually, it was sweet pudding or some dumb shit that fell from his lips. What he didn't know was I would play his little game with him just so I could have a reason to leave and willingly jump on Zamir's dick again. The very moment Joseph slipped up and let me even get a whiff of him cheating, I was gone leave faster than a crackhead who just got their next hit.

"What's up, Joseph. Hello." I extended my hand to the girl, and she shook it.

"Denver, this is Raquel. Raquel, this is Denver," Joseph introduced us.

I gave her a small smile and sat my ass back down. His parents walked in the house, eyes glossy as hell, and smiled at him.

"Oh, praise the Lord. Raquel, baby, it's nice to see you," his mother yelled, pulling her into a hug.

Letting out a small chuckle, I shook my head. This lady was really doing all this Lord talk and was high. Mary Wells looked over at me and released Raquel. She was trying to play it safe with me, and it was only because I held her dirty little secret. Joseph asked were we all ready, and everyone said yes. We walked outside and went to the cars, and this bitch had the nerve to walk to the front seat of this man's car, like I was about to ride in the back, and his punk ass opened the door for her.

"Joseph, you can sit here and play with me if you want to. I will beat your ass out here. Now, whatever little games you and miss thing here got going on don't need to be played in my face. So, let me know now who the fuck is she, where the fuck she came from, and why she thinks she 'bout to sit in the front seat while your girlfriend is going to sit in the back." Placing my hand on my hip, I waited for him to speak.

Joseph's ass was used to the nice me, the proper me. He ain't know shit about the drug slinging, gun toting, firecracker I was, but his ass was gone find out today if he kept his bullshit up.

"Denver, honey, calm down. Raquel is my best friend. She's the girl that was my first love as a child. She has been away for two years in the army." He smiled at her so lovingly.

"Oh, okay, I'll do you one better. Y'all have a great night. I'm gone go on home. Don't bother to call me when she leaves again." I waved goodbye, and Joseph ran behind me.

"I didn't mean to make you uncomfortable. I would really like if you joined us all. You are my girlfriend, and I just wanted you two to meet each other. I'm sorry if I went about it the wrong way. Please forgive me," he begged.

"You're good, I'm out." I climbed in my car and pulled off, not giving a fuck about what he said.

I was going to play his game a little longer just so I could grab some extra clientele. The way his mom was snorting that shit up her nose, I knew she would be big money. That also would give me access to all the druggies in the church. Now I wouldn't take nothing up inside the church, but if the pastor wanted a hit, he could meet my ass a few blocks down. Driving straight to my grandma's house, I used my key to let myself in. Walking further into the house, I felt my tears build up. Walking into her room, it was the exact same way she left it. Going over to her bed, I got on my knees and prayed. I prayed for my family by name, and I asked my grandma to help guide me in the right direction. I asked her to watch over my Dakota and to send me a sign that they were alright. After I was done, I got up and laid in her bed.

My grandma's scent was strong, so the smell in her bed was as if she was sitting right there. I closed my eyes and drifted off to sleep.

⚜

The ringing of my phone caused me to jump up. Looking over at the nightstand, I saw it was now ten the next morning. I hadn't even known I slept the night away. Climbing out of my grandma's bed, I made it back the way she had left it. I slowly walked to my old room, glad that I still had clothes here. Grabbing a cute sundress, bra, and some sandals, I took a shower. My ass wasn't wearing no panties today. My plans were to somehow run into Za and fuck his ass. His dick was immaculate. I'd only had two in my life, but his was the best. The way he licked my spine while hitting it from the back was some shit that just wouldn't leave my mind. I wanted more of him in the worst way.

Leaving the house, I headed to one of the spots to pick up money. We hadn't opened our trap houses back up, but the boys were still getting to the money by any means, and I loved it. I also found myself bringing my laptop with me a whole lot and sitting outside of each one of their houses for hours, watching who came in and out. What fucked me up was I didn't see any foul shit, making it hard to believe a snake was on the team. Pulling up to one of the houses ten minutes later, I grabbed my gun, cocked it, placed it on my thigh strap, and got out the car. I made my way to the house Shizz stayed in and went inside.

"What's up, baby girl, I hear you stepping down." He licked his lips at me.

"Yeah, the person whose spot it rightfully is, is back now. I'm putting all my focus into school. Graduating college is important," I replied and was serious.

Hell, I didn't even know how I was passing when my attendance wasn't the best. However, I did all my work and passed all my tests so far. Shizz nodded and handed me the brown envelope. I stuck it in my back and was on my way. I got in my car and pulled off. Auntie's house wasn't too far, and I wanted to go by and check on things and see if anything was different.

I sang Monica songs the whole way there and when I got out, I walked to the door and looked around. I felt like somebody was watching me. Instead of going inside, I walked back down the steps. Before I could reach my car, shots rang out. I didn't even know where they were coming from. Ducking down beside the car, I pulled my gun out and looked around. The window on the car I was on the side of broke and shattered over top of me. My heart was pounding and for the first time, I was second guessing getting into this shit. I had never been in a shootout before or even had anyone shooting at me. I always did the shooting. There was no time to call anyone, so I had to handle this the best way that I could. There was no doubt about it that Zamir and Manny could have this shit. I wasn't trying to die or get shot. I crawled to the next car and stood up, shooting across the street into the alley since that was directly across from me. I could see the figure trying to duck behind the wall, but I wasn't stopping until my clip was empty, and I had a ladder clip.

I kept shooting, and I knew one of my shots landed because I saw him fall. Running to my car, I jumped in and sped off. Manny had told me he had to stop by his mom's, so I headed there doing way over the speed limit. I didn't stop until I made it there. Jumping out the car, I ran inside and locked the door. Hearing Manny yell about his feelings made me slow my pace. I walked deeper into the house and was stuck for a second. I knew damn well he wasn't messing with Justine and didn't tell me. This bitch found my brother but didn't bother looking for me or even giving me a heads up that she was leaving. Instead of making myself known, I stood off to the side watching everything unfold.

29

JUSTINE

God had to be saying fuck me in the worst way. I thought my crying was done, and after what Blu did to me, I had been able to stay out of his way and had been in a hotel room for the past month. It took a lot out of my savings, but it was worth it. My car was now put on the back burner and searching for a new apartment wasn't going as planned. Today was the seventh day I had been feeling like a truck hit me. My body was sore, my nipples hurt, and every night I would be up bent over the trash can. I just knew that God was trying to sit my ass down before I even really got started. Running to the Walgreens across the street, I went ahead and grabbed two pregnancy tests and then went into the dollar store to grab three more. I had read somewhere on social media that the dollar store had the best ones. Going back inside my hotel room, I texted Trish to see how far away she was. And when she replied twenty minutes, I knew I had enough time since I was already dressed. Taking each test out, I followed the instructions and took them one by one.

After washing my hands, I walked back and forth around the room. I knew that if I was having a baby, I needed to change. Sex for money would have to go on just until I started showing. The hotel thing would be over, and every day I would do the foot work to finding a place. I had already gotten my landlord to change my locks, and since Blu's schedule didn't change, I would move around him just to stay away from him. Because going to the cops wouldn't help me, especially when he had been on the force for years and was highly favored.

Going back into the bathroom and looking at each test, I dropped to my knees and cried. My ass was having a baby. The thing that was most fucked up was I didn't have a single clue as to who the baby belonged to. If it went my way, it would be Manny's child. Everything with him was perfect to me, and even with it being early in our little situation, I knew he would be the perfect dad since he was the perfect man to me. Tossing all the tests in the trash, I walked outside just as Trish was pulling up. Climbing into her car, she gave me a soft smile and pulled off. The entire ride was silent. A few stores in the mall were having a sale and she wanted me to go with her since her daughter was busy. So, when we pulled up to a nice ass house, I was confused.

"Girl, come on. Ain't nobody home and I forgot my wallet. It's hot as hell out here, and you shouldn't be waiting in the car." Trish shut her car off and climbed out.

Following behind her, I stepped into her home and looked around in awe. When I saw the picture of Manny, her, and her husband on the wall, I smiled. They were a beautiful family and the love they had for each other could be seen in the picture. Trish walked up the spiral stairs while I looked around the house. After a few minutes, she came back down and wrapped her arms around me. We shared a kiss, and she slid her tongue in my mouth.

"Ma, you got my—what the fuck is going on?" Manny yelled.

I put my head down in shame while his mom smiled at him and the Greek god he was with. That man was tall and beyond fine. If I could I climb him and ride his face, I would. Yet, that was a quick thought that left when I looked over at Manny, who had an unreadable expression on his face.

"Manny, stop, you know how ya dad and I get down. I just so happen to like this one a little more than the girls of the past. Y'all wasn't 'pose to meet, so don't tell your dad. His ass a be mad I'm getting some pussy without him." She shrugged and grabbed my hand, but my feet wouldn't move.

Trish looked between Manny and me, and now she wore a frown.

"So, you're doing it like that, Justine?" he asked me, voice so low I barely heard him.

"Justine? Her name is Lisa," his mom replied. Only if she knew she was making it worse.

"So, you a liar too? Who are you, huh? You got me out here looking like a whole bitch behind you. I was there for you, whatever you fucking needed, I had you. Let me ask you this, though, Lisa or whoever the hell you want to be. Did you know you was fucking me and my parents?" he asked me calmly while licking his lips.

I guess me not answering told it all, because before anybody could react, his ass was across the kitchen. My ass wasn't slow, so I ran into the bathroom I had found when I first was looking around, and locked the door. Sliding down the wall, I cried here for not only myself but my unborn child. I knew now that providing for him or her wouldn't be as easy as I thought. I could hear Manny on the other side breathing heavy like he ran a mile. Being as though I was pregnant, I wouldn't fight him or even go into a screaming contest with him. My ass wasn't prepared for the storm I knew was brewing on the other side of the door.

"You really gone do me like that. I finally was ready to settle down, and with you. Man, something was telling me stay away from your ass, but I couldn't. For the first time in a while, shit felt right. I was content with sleeping with you at night and always looked forward to talking to your ass throughout the day. Look how that turned out for me. Is Justine your real name? Were you gone tell me what was going on? Please, let me know what's up," Manny spoke through the door.

Easing up off the floor and wiping my tears, I felt like I owed him an explanation. Manny made me feel what no one had ever done, and I was kind of fucked up for messing that up. Opening the bathroom door, I stepped right into his hand. He grabbed me by the neck and held me against the wall.

"Emmanuel, please let me go." I struggled to get out of his hold.

"I should fucking kill you, bro. I ain't ever let a bitch play me," he hissed, squeezing tighter.

Where the hell were his mom and Mr. Fine Ass at when I needed them? Clawing at his hands, my eyes began to roll. And he let me go, tossing me to the floor like a rag doll.

"I'm sorry, okay, my life was fucked up and I was just trying to survive. I didn't mean to hurt you. I met you after your parents and I had already done what we did. The money was good and I needed it. I found out who you were to them and I was being selfish, trying to protect myself. The damage is already done and I hope I can fix it," I got out while holding my neck.

"That don't fucking matter. The moment you found out, you should have fucking told me," he snapped, flipping the table that was in the hall. It just missed my head. Jumping up, I got ready to fight him.

"I ain't about to stand here and just let you beat my ass. Yeah, what I did was fucked up, but I'm not gone let you physically hurt me," I told him, and he stormed over to me.

"Bitch, on my momma, the way I'm feeling, you don't want these problems," he growled, and I swung, knocking him in the mouth. I kept on swinging, letting out all the pain from everyone who had hurt me. I punched him for what Blu did to me and for what he himself said to me.

At first Manny wasn't swinging back, but one good hit to the mouth had him slapping fire from my ass. I fell into the wall and before I could get my footing right, he snatched me up by my hair and placed his gun to the side of my head.

"Manny, you better not." Trish's ass finally decided to step in.

"Why somebody just was shooting at me?" I knew her voice from anywhere, it was Denver.

Tall and sexy's head snapped to her, and the look on his face went from amusement to like he was about to kill us all.

"Justine, what the fuck? Bitch, I been looking for you everywhere. Manny, what are you doing?" Denver tried to get to me but was held back.

He ignored her and continued with me. "Give me one reason why I shouldn't kill you," he said, close enough to kiss me.

"Because I'm pregnant," I cried. Trish sucked in a breath, and he dropped the gun to his side and walked off. Denver looked at me, confused, and I ran out the door. I stopped in my tracks as a group of masked men started up the steps. Turning around to run back in the house, the next words that were said had me looking over my shoulder, hand on the doorknob, frozen.

"You led me right to them." Blu smirked with a deranged look on his face.

Made in the USA
Columbia, SC
01 September 2021

44704977R00105